ONE SWEET DAY IS NEVER ENOUGH

ONE SWEET DAY BOOK TWO

JILLIAN WALSH

One Sweet Day is Never Enough

Copyright © 2020 by Jillian Walsh.

All Rights Reserved.

All rights reserved under International and Pan American Copyright conventions. No part of this book may be reproduced, transmitted, downloaded, recorded, or stored in any information storage and retrieval system, in any form or by any means, whether electronic or mechanical, now known or hereinafter invented, without the express written permission of the publisher, except for brief quotations for review purposes.

This is a work of fiction. Names, characters, places, and incidents are products of the author's imagination or are used fictitiously and are not to be construed as real. Any resemblance to actual events, locales, organizations, or persons, living or dead, is entirely coincidental.

First Edition, 2020

ONE

Eyes on the prize, Stewart. I need you to get this right. The voice of Gia's boss, Noreen Jenkins, echoed through her brain.

A bundle of nerves, Gia Stewart leaned in to study some merchandise at the market situated on the Pederson Cherry Orchard and Winery. She'd arrived too early for her afternoon appointment with the owner.

Feeling restless, browsing the charming little store seemed like the only sensible option. Gia read a label on a jar of jam three times, failing to recall what it said, and set it back on the shelf, too preoccupied to care.

Maybe her eyes were a little *too* focused on the prize? She needed to settle down, for crying out loud. She scolded herself and took a deep breath.

She'd recently botched a few aspects of the first wedding assignment for the agency she'd been working for since April, however, although everything had worked out in the end. But she was on shaky ground, and Noreen didn't parse words. It was time to find out if Gia would "sink or swim."

Gia switched her weight from one heeled, sandaled foot to the other and transferred her gaze to another shelf. She tapped a jar of apricot chutney with her perfectly manicured pink nails and checked her watch—twenty more minutes.

Her gaze wandered around the orchard's shop. Colorful scented candles. Instrumental music. Very soothing.

It wasn't as though she hadn't met with venue owners to go over party details before. Gia had worked in event planning for two years and had just completed an online event planning certification.

Still, this appointment doubled as a sales call, and she wasn't very savvy when it came to sales, even if she'd be pitching to someone no more intimidating than a hardworking cherry farmer. Still, if Gia could bring Mr. Pederson on board with holding nuptials on his property consistently from May through October, it would be the first step toward reinstating Gia in the role from which she'd recently been downgraded with her agency. She sighed. *One step at a time.*

It was time to stop being such a nervous Nellie. She picked up a jar of fiery-hot salsa from a shelf and turned it over to glance at the ingredients. *You can do this.*

"Can I help you?" Startled, Gia set the salsa down at the sound of a friendly male voice. She spun around to face the clerk and felt a flutter in her stomach. The guy was ruggedly handsome, tall with broad shoulders and closely cropped, brown hair.

She straightened her long green skirt and white ruffled top, switching the folder she held under one arm to the other. "Oh, hi. Sure, that would be great."

He must've just come in because she would've spotted him if he'd been there for a while. He wasn't the type of guy who walked across a room unnoticed. He *was* the type of guy who made her forget everything she'd just been thinking about. Quick—what to say? She made her voice sound casual. "I, uh... I thought I'd send something local home to my parents in Minneapolis. What do you suggest?"

He glanced at the shelf. "Oh, okay. Let's see. Maybe some jam? My mother's a big fan of this one. He pulled down a jar and held it out for her to see. "We do our own canning right here on the farm."

Gia nodded, trying to keep from staring at his perfect jawline. She took the jar from him and smiled politely. "Okay, thanks. This is great." It would also be great if she could keep the dumb grin from taking over her entire face.

The last thing she needed right now was a distraction, no matter how good-looking, especially when she had so much on the line, but one look into those piercing brown eyes and she could hardly look away. She forced her gaze back to the jar of jam. "Cherry apple. Yes, they'll love it. Thank you."

He nodded, and she stole another glance at him. In black denims and work boots, he had the look of a man who could take an axe to one of the cherry trees outside and not even break a sweat. Yet the way he carried himself lent him an air of sophistication, too. Very appealing.

Still, she was here on a professional matter. She'd be meeting with the man who was probably this handsome stud's boss. It wouldn't look good if she were flirting with the staff.

She cleared her throat, tearing her gaze from the muscular tone of his shoulders, not easily disguised by the starched, short-sleeved gray button-down he was wearing. "Do you think I could I ask you for a favor?"

He nodded, slipping a hand into the pocket of his jeans. "Sure."

"Thanks. I have an appointment with Mr. Pederson at two thirty, and I'm a bit early." She glanced at her watch. "But it's just about that time now. Would you let him know I'm here? I wasn't told exactly where to find him."

A look of surprise crossed his face, and he relaxed. "Actually, you're looking at him. I'm Seth Pederson. My father's the owner."

Gia blushed. "Oh, I shouldn't have assumed...I'm so sorry." She was told she'd be meeting with John Pederson, a man in his late sixties.

He offered a hand. "It's no problem. I get that a lot lately. You must be with the Jenkins Agency?"

"Uh, yes, I am." She took his hand, and he shook it warmly. "Gia Stewart."

"Great, Gia. Yes, I'll be meeting with you today."

Gia nodded, hoping the pink in her cheeks was fading because the heat certainly was not. "I see. Well, it's great to meet you."

"Likewise. I moved back home recently to help with the family business. My dad... Actually, judging from your question, I'm assuming no one told your agency about my dad's condition?"

Gia shook her head slowly.

"My dad suffered a heart attack in April. He's home and doing better, but he won't be back up to speed for quite some time, so I've taken over."

"Oh, my goodness. No, we didn't know. I'm so sorry to hear that."

"Thank you. It's been a bit hectic around here without him at the helm, as you can imagine. I'm sure we have plenty of business partners that we haven't had the chance to tell. I apologize."

"Oh, I completely understand. I'll make sure Noreen knows."

"I'd appreciate that. Nothing will change in regard to the anniversary party, by the way. Everything's still on."

She nodded. That was a relief. "Okay, well that's great to hear. We're excited to make it happen." He clapped his hands together and then rubbed them back and forth. "So would you like to see more of the property? I can show you the venue outside."

"Yes, that would be great." Gia followed him to the door. "Oh, but wait, I need to pay for this." She held up the jar of jam.

Seth waved it away. "Oh, no, don't worry about it."

Gia grinned. "Really? Are you sure? I don't mind."

"Really." He seemed sincere. "Consider it a gift—cherry-apple jam for our new event planner. Well, for her mother, I guess?"

Gia blushed again. "Well, all right, if you say so. Thank you so much." She put the jar into her handbag. It would be rude to refuse at that point, wouldn't it?

Gia remembered, having scanned the guest list this morning, that Mr. and Mrs. Pederson, as well as a Seth Pederson, were all actually invited to the party she'd be planning. It wasn't surprising though, since the Pederson Orchard was practically an icon of the local cherry-farming industry. The fiftieth wedding anniversary party, after all, was being thrown for an iconic couple involved in the local sportfishing industry, Tim and Abigail Trewet. Of course they would know each other.

She wondered if the Trewets knew about Mr. Pederson's health condition, however. She made a mental note to ask Abigail when they spoke next.

Seth held the door for Gia. "Noreen's email said Jackie did all the plans. So why did they hand the event over to you? Not that I mind."

Gia smiled and thanked him, squinting as they walked outside. "Noreen was just switching some things around and thought I'd be well-suited here. She put Jackie on a big wedding. We're triple-booked that night." She gave a little flip to her long, light-blonde hair. It was the only part of the story he needed to hear, and she didn't want him losing faith in her from the get-go. "But don't worry. I've done this plenty of times. You're in good hands." *Or so I hope.*

"Oh, I'm not worried." Seth rested his hands casually in his pockets.

That makes one of us. She felt her shoulders stiffen up.

He gestured for her to go first as they entered a tailored lawn surrounded by a wall of short, well-kept hedges and set off by rows of pink impatiens and white alyssum. An arbor festooned with climbing roses stood at the far end in full bloom. Two leafy trees shaded one corner of the spacious yard.

Seth held out his arms. "So this is where we hold our events."

Gia strolled across the yard to get a feel for the size of it. It was perfect. Large enough to accommodate a big event but still, intimate enough. She nodded with satisfaction.

A gleaming red barn and a silo stood on the other side of a wide driveway that led to a second parking lot. A vineyard stood just past the lot, and beyond, fields of cherry trees on three sides. But only the portion of the orchard nearest the barn looked leafy and green.

She gazed at the setting, trying not to reveal her concern

at the withered appearance of so many of the trees farther off in the distance. "Quite an operation you've got here."

Seth grinned. "I'll take that as a compliment."

Gia flashed a smile. "Yes, I meant it that way."

He sighed. "Thanks. And you're right. My dad's had his hands full. Seventy-five acres of cherries, five acres of berry patches and apple trees, and twenty acres of grapes." Seth pointed to the vineyard and then motioned toward the barn. "The wine-tasting room and the barrel room are inside. So yeah, there's always something that needs doing around here."

"I can imagine. It's stunning, by the way. I can't wait to see the lawn all dressed up for the party."

"Thanks. Me, too. My parents put a lot of money into renovations for the barn and a few other things last fall after the harvest. A lot of it still looks new."

"It really does." Gia pulled some documents out of her folder and studied them. A more senior planner had put the initial arrangements in place, and then Gia had taken over. "I've got Jackie's plans here." She pointed across the yard. "It looks like the catering tent will go over there, the stage and the dance floor, over here."

Seth moved closer to look over her shoulder. She could smell the fresh-but-subtle scent of his cologne—a tantalizing ocean breeze. She inhaled deeply and hoped he didn't notice.

He glanced at the plans and out at the yard. "Okay, so yeah, the setup looks good. There's plenty of room for all the dining tables and the service aisle. And the client hired a band, right?"

"Yes."

"Okay, great." He walked out farther into the grass. "So I've been thinking. I'd like to start looking at doing weddings and other big events here, at full capacity whenever possible, which is just over four hundred guests. I have another event space inside the winery, too, for smaller gatherings." He pointed at the barn then turned to Gia. "Can you can talk to Noreen about that, or should I give her a call?"

Gia's eyebrows shot up. "Wait—you want to do weddings on a regular basis? Big ones? And you have space in your barn, too?"

"Yeah. Do you think that's possible? I can talk to another agency if you're not in the position to take on more—"

"Oh no. No, don't do that!" Gia stopped him. "It's completely possible." She let out a heavy breath. "It's funny, because I was going to ask you if you'd be interested in something like that today. Noreen was hoping you might be." *To say the least.*

It was time to lay on her full sales pitch, and get it over with, especially while her subject was warm. She pasted a smile on her face. "We've always got a lot of brides looking for outdoor spaces like this, especially in the summer—wineries, cider mills, orchards. We can keep you fairly busy with events if you're interested?"

Could it be that easy? She held her breath.

He nodded. "Yeah, I'm very interested."

"Fantastic." She nodded eagerly. "Would you be open to some last-minute scheduling this season, seeing as it's already July? Now and then an overly ambitious client comes along who wants to plan an event in a few weeks, and it would be great if we could offer them your space. I can't promise you anything immediately, but it's good to know if you'd be ready and willing?"

Seth nodded again. "Absolutely. I want to go big. Whatever we can do." He looked out into the distance and pointed toward the orchard. "We suffered some serious losses this spring with the cold snap that came through late in the season. The trees were already blooming—and that's a terrible time to get hit with subzero temperatures."

"Oh, that's awful." So that explained the unhealthy look of a large part of the orchard.

She did remember the arctic blast that hit the area right after she moved to Door County, after everyone thought the winter was over. That, on its own, wasn't unusual for this part of the country, but the extreme temperatures it brought, which lasted for days, had done a number on the agricultural industry across the region.

Still, she was having a hard time keeping a handle on her excitement. Noreen was going to be thrilled. He'd not only agreed to do weddings, he wanted to do bigger ones, and he had a winery space in which to hold even more events. Furthermore, she was going to be spending more time with this perfect gentleman—lucky break.

Gia frowned at herself. Theirs would be strictly a professional relationship. No distractions. *Eyes on the prize, Stewart.* He went on and Gia refocused her attention.

"In the meantime, I'm hoping we can make up for those losses as quickly as possible with events. I need to lock down some new sources of revenue as soon as possible."

Gia nodded eagerly. "That's music to my ears. You know, we might be able to squeeze in some family reunion dinners or corporate picnics fairly soon, if you're open to those, and then get some weddings on your calendar for the fall. And next summer, of course."

Seth held up a fist. "Bring it on. Let's see what we can do."

Gia smiled big. "Absolutely."

TWO

Seth nodded and motioned for her to follow him toward the barn. He was relieved the agency would be willing and able to help. Things were getting tight around the farm, and apparently, it had been going on for the last few years, although his father hadn't told him. He'd been shocked to see just how bad things were once he'd finally gotten a look at the books.

Yet he was pleased that the event planner they'd sent to run the anniversary party seemed so competent and enthusiastic. He hadn't expected her to be so attractive, though. Not that he should be noticing since he still had a girlfriend, but he'd have to be *dead* not to.

Hopefully, Gia's event-planning strategy would be the break they needed. His father's health was improving, fortunately, but the harvest could be dismal compared to past years. His mother had been distracted with worry, understandably. It had all taken its toll on them.

Still, it was best if he didn't think for too long about those things. He should focus on fixing what he could. He was in charge of keeping this place afloat now. Wallowing in self-pity wouldn't get him anywhere, and a bright smile like Gia's was doing wonders for his mood.

"Come on. I'll show you the barrel room. We remodeled it a few years ago. It'll be a great place to hold events as soon as I take care of the proper permits."

"Okay, great." Gia fell in beside him. "So what does the rest of your summer schedule look like?"

Seth took a quick moment to run through it in his head. "Let's see: July. Other than the cherry festival next weekend and the anniversary party, we're only booked with some group reservations in the tasting room here and there. But those are all daytime hours."

The family's vineyard grew a small variety of grapes, which were shipped to a local growers' co-op to produce and bottle one white and two red wines under the Pederson label.

But like so many orchards throughout Door County, it also churned some of its own fruit into libations. Any visitor to the peninsula expected to try a chilled glass of cherry wine. The drink had become a staple, for the tourists, especially.

Gia put the documents back inside the folder as she walked alongside him. "Okay, well, I'll see what I can do and get back to you as soon as possible."

He nodded. "Sounds good. I look forward to it."

Gia cast a curious sideways glance at him as they walked. "You said you moved home recently. I'm curious as to where you were living before you moved back, if you don't mind me asking?"

"Sure, I don't mind at all. I was in Sonoma." He was pleased she wanted to know. His time there already seemed like a lifetime ago, in some ways.

"Oh, wow," Gia chirped, "California's a long way from home."

"Yeah, no kidding. I loved it there, but—you know, I'm really glad to be home. I didn't realize how much I missed it here."

Growing up on the orchard had given him the perfect education on what hard work and responsibility could do for the soul. It had given him the confidence to keep moving forward, something that came in handy when it came time to uproot his life and race home to take care of the family farm.

The peaceful setting of the trees and the fields also gave him a sense of calm in a world full of urgency and stress. He wouldn't have traded living and working at the orchard and winery for anything. He was glad to be back.

He fidgeted with a set of keys that he'd pulled from a pocket and glanced up as they reached the front of the barn. A sign overhead read "Tasting Room".

"It's only open Friday through Sunday, daytime. We can have guests arrive as early as five for weddings and such, same as the lawn venue, unless there's a special request." He fit the key in the lock and turned.

She nodded. "Okay. Perfect. So what were you doing out in California?"

He was glad she wanted to chat. Lately, it felt like the only person around to talk to was himself. "Thanks for asking. I got my degree in business administration from Sonoma State. They offer a certificate in wine management. Got that, too."

He pushed open the heavy door. "Then I went to work for one of the busy wineries out there. They're well known in that region, but you probably haven't heard of them out here—the Henderson Estates?"

She shook her head.

"They're only selling locally and in-state at this point. Great wine, but not a big name. Anyway, I learned a lot—growing, pouring, tasting, production. I was in management when I left."

"That sounds so exciting. You must've loved it."

He had. Not that he'd had the time to think much about it lately, but yeah, it had been the opportunity of a lifetime. He nodded agreeably. "I really did."

He'd left his girlfriend behind in Sonoma, too. Stacey Lochner had worked at the Henderson Estates with him as a wine-tasting attendant. He'd left in such a rush after his father's heart attack that he hadn't really processed what would become of them as a couple after he left. But they were still together. If you could call it being *together* when there were two thousand miles between them and so many important conversations about their future left unspoken.

He dismissed the thoughts. There was enough to worry about lately with the farm and his father. Why worry about *that*—when it only made his stomach turn?

Seth held the door for Gia, and she stepped into the renovated barn. The air was cool and smelled faintly of grapes with a rich oaky undertone. He switched on a couple of low lights and led Gia past the tasting counter, a beautiful plank of wood that had been varnished to a glossy finish and ran the full length of one wall. Several seating areas with tables were clustered about the room and a door led to patio seating out back.

"The wine cellar's in a storage room around the other side."

Gia nodded.

He stopped in front of a set of double doors and searched for the right key. "You know, I've only been back since April, and it's great to be home, but it wasn't easy to leave it all behind. As much as I love the countryside, I'd forgotten how quiet this place really is. There were always so many people around at the Henderson Estates to talk to. This place is almost *too* quiet." He forced a grin and sighed. "It's been an adjustment."

"I'm sure it has." Gia tilted her head. "You must miss those people."

What had gotten into him? Why was he opening up to her? She was a perfect stranger and a business associate. Still, it felt good to talk about something other than business. She seemed about his age, and she seemed interested. "I do." But enough about him. "So have you moved around a lot, too?"

"Yeah, actually I have." She nodded. "I'm from Minneapolis. Went to school and worked there for a while, then I took a job in Milwaukee, and now, here I am. I like to try out new places. The world's a big place—so much to see. So far, Heritage Bay's been my favorite." She grinned. "I love the small-town vibe."

"I totally get that. So how long have you been here?"

"I actually moved here in April, too, for the job, but I know what you mean about relocating. It's easier said than done."

"You've got that right." He nodded. "Oh, hey, so you live over in Heritage Bay?"

She nodded back.

"Great place."

"It is. I really love it. And it's fairly close to the office in Anderson Cove."

The Pederson's farm was only three miles inland from the beautiful lakefront village of Heritage Bay, located about halfway up the peninsula, overlooking the picturesque waters of upper Green Bay. Anderson Cove was the next village up the coast.

"Then we're practically neighbors." He liked the thought of her living nearby. It would be much easier to work out event details if they could meet in person. She was warm and friendly, and it would be nice to talk to someone other than his parents or his employees, even if it were about business.

"So then, you left California when your dad got sick?"

He nodded.

"Did you plan to return to Wisconsin someday, anyway?"

He directed his attention to the thick rustic doors and put the key in the lock. "Okay, I think you might be reading my mind now." He turned the doorknobs and pushed. It had been a long time since someone seemed genuinely interested in hearing about his life story. "So yeah, my plan all along was to get the experience there and put it all to use here. It was always understood that I'd be taking over the family business at some point."

Gia nodded.

His younger brother and sister had pursued other things in life, and they didn't live locally, although they'd come to help out while his dad was in the hospital.

And the pull of his family's legacy on the farm was strong. It was his duty to honor it and make sure the business continued to be family-run. Moreover, they were already in the red. He had his work cut out for him.

"So yeah, when our trees were hit this spring and then my dad was rushed to the hospital, I knew it was time. I couldn't leave my mother to deal with it all. I decided to call it quits and leave Sonoma a year or two earlier than planned."

"Wow, that must've been hard." Gia pushed some hair behind her ear, exposing the smooth, flawless skin of her neck, and he looked away and turned the key in the lock. "I'll bet your father appreciates it," she said. "Your mother, too?"

"Yeah, they do. They're good people." She was so sweet. Seth let go and stepped inside the room, then turned to Gia in the doorway with a look of apology. He sighed. "I don't know why I'm laying all of this on you. You didn't ask to hear about my life—or my problems."

Gia tilted her head to the side and shot him a guilty look. "Actually, I kind of did."

He chuckled softly. "Okay. That's fair."

She nodded.

"It seems like all I'm dealing with these days are paperwork and trees." He rolled his eyes and sighed. *And a long-distance girlfriend who I don't even miss anymore.* Something had to be wrong with him when it came to Stacey. But he wouldn't tell Gia about that. He'd already unloaded enough about his personal life, and she might think he was being unprofessional.

"I can imagine." Gia smiled at him and their eyes met for a moment.

She was really gorgeous, but he shouldn't be thinking about that. He forced his gaze away and looked around for the light switch. He lit the room then motioned for her to come in. "Okay, so this is the barrel room."

Gia peered up at the twenty-foot ceilings. The center of the large space was open in the middle and surrounded on three sides by oak barrels full of aging wine stacked to the ceiling. The floors were a dramatic hardwood with a rustic finish. Soft, recessed lighting gave the room an intimate feel. He had to admit—it was an inviting backdrop for a banquet.

"This is lovely," she said. "I can totally imagine some tables set up in here with a small dance floor, maybe down this end." She pointed. "It's such a unique setting."

"Exactly. Thanks. I think it has a lot of potential."

"So how long has the barn been here? It looks old and historically accurate, but it feels brand new."

"You're right. It is." Again, how cool was this woman? She noticed exactly the kinds of things he did. They were so fortunate to have her on the job. "The original barn was built in the 1940s. It was falling apart, so we finally tore it down and built a new one to look just like the old one about twenty years ago. But instead of using it as a traditional barn, we dedicated it all to the wine. My parents just had it jazzed up last fall with all the finishing touches and a new coat of paint. My dad's been trying to grow the winery business for me because he knows that's my favorite part of the operation."

"Wow. That's wonderful."

"Thanks. My dad's a great guy, and the orchard's been in our family for four generations. He wanted to make his mark by starting the winery."

"Really? That's incredible. You've got a lot on your shoulders with that kind of history."

He stopped and smiled at her. That thought ran through his head almost every day.

"I really love it in here." Gia glanced around the room. "Noreen will be excited to offer it to our clients."

Seth nodded. "Fantastic."

They shared a relaxed silence for a few moments as Gia gazed at different features of the room. She jotted down a few notes in her folder.

"I can get you the exact square footage later, and anything else you might need when I get back to my office."

"That would be great. So did the cold weather damage your vineyard, too?"

Seth shoved his hands inside the front pockets of his pants again. "Two of the grape varieties withstood the temperature flux pretty well, so we're okay on that, and we're still well stocked from last fall, so we'll be all right. Plus, we import some wines from other states for the tasting room—Michigan, Vermont, California."

Gia nodded. "I see. Well, that's good."

"Oh, and we can offer our own wines for parties, in addition to whatever the clients want to have brought in."

"Okay, perfect, I'll make a note of that."

Seth straightened his shoulders and looked her in the eye. "So the thing is, I've got a lot of work ahead of me to make this place profitable again. Right now, we're hanging on, and cherry-picking season begins this weekend, but I'd like to get things started quickly on the events. So what's our next step to make that happen?"

Gia nodded. "I hear you. I'll talk to Noreen to see if you need any other licensing. Can you email me and let me know what you've already taken care of?"

"Sure."

"And then I'll find out if she's got any clients looking for a place like this right now." She gazed at him. "We'll do our best to make it quick. I'm so glad you've come to us with this, Mr. Pederson. I'll get the paperwork drawn up as soon as possible."

"That sounds great." He gazed warmly at her. "And please—call me Seth."

"Thank you. In the meantime, I'll contact you about the anniversary party if any questions come up." She reached into her bag. "Here's my card if you think of anything else.

You can also email me the details you mentioned regarding the barn."

He took the card. "I'll do that."

"Thanks for the tour." She offered a hand.

He shook it. "Absolutely. Thank *you*. It's been a pleasure." Those deep-blue eyes of hers were something else.

Seth felt a buzz in the back pocket of his jeans. He grabbed his phone and looked at the screen. Stacey—again. He had just talked to her an hour ago. He silenced the call and glanced at Gia apologetically. "Sorry."

"Oh, it's no problem." Gia waved it off. "I've got to get back to the office. I'll be in touch."

THREE

Gia pulled into a local diner style restaurant after work, exhausted. She was meeting friends for dinner. What a day. Noreen was satisfied with her after she'd reported on her meeting at the orchard. She'd been thrilled about the winery venue and said she'd start the paperwork to get the ball rolling first thing tomorrow. At least Noreen was happy with her about that.

Despite her worry, the sales call with Seth had gone well. Gia let out a sigh of relief—all that anxiety for nothing. It would make the weekend's wedding fiasco easier to put behind her, at least, and she'd be sure to cross every *t* and dot every *i* from now on. There was no more room for mistakes.

She found the group inside the restaurant and sat down in the booth next to Kira. Courtney slipped in across the seat from them. Courtney's boyfriend, Nick slid in next to Courtney. The diner was cheap and fast and the booths were large enough to fit six of them at once, if not more.

Nick's roommate, Tom, walked up to the table amidst

the chatter and laughter. "Slide over, sister." He grinned. "Unless you want me to sit on your lap."

Gia smiled. "I'm sliding." She slid over and patted at the seat next to her.

Tom squeezed in, greeted everyone, and rubbed shoulders with Gia. "Good to see you. How've ya been?"

Tom Garcia was good-looking at six foot one with short dark hair, friendly, brown eyes and a slim-but-muscular build. He was also very good-natured and had quickly become one of Gia's favorite people in Heritage Bay. They'd met at a party on the Fourth of July, and she and Tom had hit it off and exchanged numbers. They regularly talked now by phone or text, but there was nothing going on between them other than a friendship.

The Fourth of July party had been rough for Courtney and Nick, who'd almost broken up for good that night. Fortunately, it looked as though that was light-years behind them now. Gia glanced across the table at the happy couple.

Courtney looked to be explaining something to him while she casually straightened a few hairs that were out of place on his head. Nick was a devoted boyfriend who couldn't seem to get enough of her. They were a match made in heaven.

Gia studied her menu, and after everyone ordered, the joking and talking resumed.

Although she'd only known Kira for a few months and Courtney a few weeks, Gia had already become close with both girls. They'd made it easier not to get homesick or miss her old friends back in Minneapolis or Milwaukee. There were two other girls, as well—Marcy and Angela—who were usually part of the group but couldn't make it tonight. Marcy was a waitress and Angela, a bartender—both, just for the summer—and both worked evenings.

Kira looked around. "So what's been going on today, kids? Anything exciting?" She rested her chin on her hand and her elbow on the table.

"Well, I rented out a unit to a new tenant today, among other things," Tom said with feigned enthusiasm. Tom was a co-manager of the apartment-and-condominium complex where he and Nick lived. "This young man will be staying for six months, minimum. Paid the full security deposit without batting an eye. How's that for an interesting day?"

Nick shot him an ironic grin. "Fascinating, dude. And I rented bicycles to about two-dozen people today. How's that for life-changing?"

Courtney turned to Nick and kissed him on the cheek. "One day not saving lives and he's bored out of his skull."

"She's right, Doctor Dreamy, not every day can be a life or death 'sitch." Tom said dryly, without disguising his amusement.

Nick and Tom volunteered as medics for the local wilderness search-and-rescue team.

"I never said it had to be life or death." Nick laughed, pretending to be sore about it.

"We know, babe." Courtney squeezed his arm. "There's always tomorrow," she said, faking pity.

"Life on the docks not quite keeping up with the Nickster's pace?" Tom regularly gave Nick a hard time, all in good fun.

Nick shook his head. "Just barely."

Courtney gave Nick another quick kiss, this time on the lips. "I'm just playing around."

He kissed her back. "I know."

"'Bout enough PDA on that side of the booth," Tom said. "Let's keep those hands on the table, kids."

Everyone laughed.

Courtney was a writer, and Kira, a photographer and videographer for the Wisconsin Visitors Board.

Gia had first met Kira back in April, not long after moving to Heritage Bay, when she was visiting a bed and breakfast property to scope it out as a potential wedding location for a bride. Kira had introduced Gia to Courtney as well as the others as they'd started arriving for the summer, and the friendship circle had grown to include Nick and Tom and another of Nick's friends, Jake, whom Angela had recently started dating. Tom mentioned that Jake had other plans tonight and couldn't make it to dinner.

"Okay, so I have some news," Gia offered.

"Oh yeah?" Courtney and Nick turned to listen.

"Finally, someone devoid of sarcasm." Kira grinned. "Go ahead, Gia." She sipped her iced tea and waited.

Gia told them about the anniversary party she'd just been assigned, downplaying the weekend's wedding mishap and the fact that an upcoming wedding had been taken away from her. Look on the bright side, her mother always said, and the world looks with you. And so she would.

"That's exciting, Gia!" Courtney leaned in.

"Thanks." Gia smiled. "Fingers crossed it goes well."

"So where's the party?" Nick asked.

"And can *we* come?" Tom joked.

"Nobody's going anywhere, Thomas," Kira said affectionately. "Now let the poor girl talk."

Gia laughed and explained. Nick and Tom said they knew of the Pederson Orchard. Kira had also been there last year with Sam, her then-boyfriend.

"Yeah, it's such a beautiful setting. I can't get over it." Gia went on to explain how the owner had agreed to host more weddings there on a regular basis and that her boss was happy with her for pulling off that feat. "The owner was really nice, too. Friendly and smart." Gia found herself with a wide grin that wouldn't go away.

"That's excellent." Kira gave her a little pat on the back. "Good job."

"Thank you." Gia looked at the group appreciatively. If they only knew how badly she needed a pat on the back.

The food arrived, and Gia dove into her fried whitefish sandwich. It turned out she wasn't only tired, she was starving.

Courtney looked at Kira. "Okay, Kira, so correct me if I'm wrong, but I haven't seen that kind of grin on Gia's face before."

Kira looked at Gia.

Gia started to blush. "What kind of grin?"

"You're right, Court." Kira eyed her suspiciously. "In fact, she seems to be glowing with excitement. So tell, tell. What else happened today, Gia?"

The guys looked interested but stayed quiet. Tom took a bite of his corned beef on rye.

"Nothing," Gia insisted. Was she that easy to read? Okay, so she'd had a nice time talking to Seth, but she'd only brought him up once—and barely. Maybe it was the fact that she couldn't stop smiling.

Courtney raised an eyebrow and dipped a French fry in ketchup then started up again. "So you mentioned the owner of the orchard and that he's friendly and smart, but what other words would you use to describe this owner?" She dropped the fry into her mouth.

Gia sucked some soda through her straw before she answered them. "Oh, come on, you guys. He's just a nice guy."

"Uh-huh." Kira grunted. "And?"

"And he's about, I don't know, twenty-seven or twenty-eight, probably."

"Uh-huh," said Courtney with more interest. "And what does he look like?"

Gia hesitated. She was trying to forget about his looks.

Tom cut in. "Come on, Stewart. We're waiting."

"Okay. Tall, dark hair..." Gia paused.

"And?" Kira asked.

How did they always manage to pull this kind of thing out of her? "Okay, he's incredibly handsome."

"There it is!" Kira smacked her hand on the table and the others laughed. "I knew it. You met a hottie."

Nick took a bite of his burger, shaking his head at them, and Tom snorted, stuffing a handful of fries into his mouth.

"Oh, stop!" Gia said, blushing. "I wouldn't call him a *hottie*."

Kira raised an eyebrow. "Why not?"

Gia glanced down at the table and spoke quietly. "Because he's too sophisticated for that word."

Kira swooned and Courtney's eyes went wide. "So what's his name?"

"It doesn't matter!" Gia protested.

Kira ate a piece of cantaloupe from the fruit salad on her plate and Courtney set down her fork. "His name, please," Courtney persisted.

Nick sat back, chuckling. "Is this how these conversations usually go?"

"All signs point to yes." Tom looked at Kira and Courtney. "Come on, ladies, give the girl a break."

Nick shook his head and went back to his burger.

Gia rested a hand on Tom's arm. "Thank you, Tom." She looked at the girls. "I'm glad someone's on my side."

Courtney was undeterred. "Seriously, we're waiting,

Gia. All you've told us this summer is how you're determined *not* to meet any more soon-to-be ex-boyfriends." Courtney crossed her hands on the table. "So you can imagine our surprise when you finally exhibit an ounce of interest in someone. When's the last time you even looked twice at a cute guy?"

"Sitting right here," Tom said, making a small circle in the air with his pointer finger.

"I've looked twice at cute guys plenty of times," she said defensively. "And you don't count, Tom. You don't treat women like most guys do." She touched his arm gently. "Although, you are cute."

Courtney was right. Gia had had so many bad experiences with men in the past that she'd all but given up on them—most of them, at least. In all of her past relationships, she'd just been too *nice*, and they'd usually rewarded her by treating her like a walking doormat. Lately, she turned down more dates than she accepted.

"Thanks, G, but how would you know?" asked Tom. "You haven't even given me a chance." He sounded sincere but she saw the teasing look in his eyes.

Gia laughed. Tom was a nice guy. They were all hoping to introduce him to some equally nice girl who would steal his heart and bring him the kind of never-ending bliss he deserved. Until then, he seemed to want to spend his time flirting with Gia.

"No, really, Gia. What's his name?" Kira was all business. "Drop the act. We want details."

"Oh, my gosh. Okay, fine! His name is Seth. He's super sweet. He moved back from California a few months ago after his father had a heart attack, and he's taken over the family business. Seems like a great businessman, but really down-to-earth, too. We talked a while. You guys would like him."

"I wouldn't," Tom said, not missing a beat.

Gia laughed. "Yes, you would."

"Seth," Tom repeated with a disdainful smirk. "Sounds like some sort of nickname for a drug problem." Tom took another bite of his sandwich, sighing loudly. It was no secret he had a thing for Gia.

"I believe you mean—" Courtney began.

"—I know what I mean." Tom scolded Courtney with a good-natured grin.

Courtney laughed and ignored him. "Well, that's what I was waiting to hear, Gia." She took a sip of her lemonade. "I'm so glad, honey. It's about time you met a nice guy. The summer's going to fly by. I want you to find your *someone*."

"Still sitting right here," Tom said.

They all chuckled.

Gia took a bite of her sandwich. Seth was more interesting than any guy who'd chatted her up this summer. But that wasn't the type of relationship they were going to have. She'd be working with him. It was strictly professional. She could not afford to screw this up. She'd better put a lid on it before her mind wandered too far.

"Well, even so, he's still a business associate. I really shouldn't even be considering what he looks like."

"Why not?" Courtney protested. "That's how Nick and I met. Right, honey?"

Nick grinned. They'd met on Courtney's first story assignment. "She was my client—sort of. On a kayak trip."

Courtney narrowed her brows. "No, you were *my* client. Sort of."

Kira rolled her eyes. "You two were so cute that day. Anyway, that's how Sam and I met, too—on the job."

Gia considered that, nodding.

"Don't encourage her, ladies. Gia is free to choose to ignore '*Meth* and date someone else."

Gia turned back to Tom and smiled facetiously. "Oh, Tom. You're always looking out for me, aren't you?"

"Don't listen to him. He's just jealous," Kira said.

"I get that a lot," Tom took a sip of his iced tea.

Nick laughed. "Tough crowd, man."

Tom rolled his eyes but looked grateful. "Blow it up, brother." Nick gave him a fist bump and they all went back to their meals.

FOUR

John Pederson, Seth's father, sat across from Seth at the dinner table. "Are we all set for the festival this weekend? I meant to ask you earlier."

"I think so." Seth wiped a napkin to his face. "I've got a few things set up besides the usual—more carnival games, pony rides, and a pie-eating contest. Enough to make it worth the visit, I'd say." The one-day festival usually saw almost a thousand visitors each year. Without as much U-Pick available, Seth was planning whatever he could to keep the public interested long enough to stay and spend a few precious dollars.

"That sounds good. We haven't done that contest in years. And the carnival games are always a hit."

Seth's mother, Clara, swallowed a bite of her chicken casserole. "Ponies sound great, and I love the pie-eating contest. Good ideas, honey."

Apparently, despite the fact that the farm wasn't turning a profit lately, last year's festival turnout had been great, and the numbers showed they'd made a good return on the U-Pick as well as on sales of merchandise and baked goods. Seth hoped they could repeat that this year. The festival was one of their biggest income-producing opportunities of the year.

Seth nodded. "Thanks. I looked at last year's numbers. How bad do you think it'll be this year with two thirds of the trees out of production?"

His father was matter-of-fact. "We can handle the hit."

Could they?

Seth's mother took a sip of her water. "It won't be the first time we've dealt with it, anyway."

"Anything I can do to help?" His father shifted in his chair.

Seth sat back. "Maybe you could run over the list of things you usually do to get ready for the festival with me tomorrow morning, just to make sure I didn't forget anything." Seth's father kept impeccable records in the office, but it wouldn't hurt to have a second set of eyes to look over the plans Seth had made over the last few weeks.

"Sure, I'd be happy to do that." His father nodded and took another bite of his green salad.

"Okay, thanks, Dad. So how'd the visit with the doctor go today?"

His mother answered for her husband. "He's got a stamp of approval on his progress—for now."

After the heart attack in early April, his father's medical team had performed an emergency angioplasty to open up his blocked blood vessels. His father had spent the next two weeks in the hospital and fortunately, had suffered only minor complications. The doctor believed that with careful monitoring, he'd eventually be able to resume some of the things he did before the heart attack.

"I'm still not allowed to exert myself, though. Not sure when I'll get the green light on *that*." He frowned.

His father valued hard work above most things, and he wasn't kidding around when he said he missed the physical labor.

Of course, he couldn't expect to do all the planting, pruning, or harvesting that he used to do. But they had farmhands for that.

"No, you most certainly are not." Seth's mother had been trying to drum it into her husband's head that he had to take it easy for a while. A stubborn, self-sufficient man all his life, his father didn't want to hear it, but at the same time, he knew things would never be the same for him. Like it or not, he was slowly accepting the idea that his son would be handling all of the day-to-day pressures of the business from now on. That had been the plan all along, whatever the case, so his father bore no resentment toward his son. He appreciated the fact that Seth had moved home and taken over.

"All in good time, Dad. All in good time."

"You've got that right." His mother looked pleased.

Seth knew his dad didn't want to be left out of the business entirely, despite his weakness at the moment, now that Seth had taken over. He also knew that his mother appreciated it when Seth kept his dad busy with things he *was* still able to do. It kept his dad feeling optimistic and useful, which were necessary for his recovery. Seth returned the grin.

After dinner, Seth said goodnight and headed down the first-floor hallway of the large family farmhouse. "I'll be in the study if anyone needs me."

"All right, dear," his mother said, loading plates into the dishwasher.

"Goodnight, son." His father pulled out the day's paper and began to skim the headlines.

At twenty-eight, Seth had made some major adjustments in his life, moving back into his parents' home after nine years in California. Leaving behind a comfortable apartment, a couple of roommates, and all the freedom in the world, not to mention a social life—it had been quite a transition.

But his mother was accommodating, and his father, grateful, when he wasn't facing one of his darker moments about the state of his health.

Seth knew he didn't have to continue with his current living situation forever, though. Maybe he'd get a place of his own if something nearby opened up, or maybe he'd build a place on the family's property.

For now, it made the most sense for him to suck it up and move back into his old bedroom on the second floor of the farmhouse.

He switched on the small desk lamp in the study, settled into the leather desk chair, then propped his laptop on the desk in front of him. He spent every waking moment working on the orchard and winery, anyway. Why add a commute?

Seth turned on the laptop for a closer look at the data from last year's harvest. A few minutes went by before his phone buzzed. He glanced at Stacey's picture as it popped up on the screen and picked up the video call, his tone flat. "Hey, what's up?"

"Hi," she said, animated. "I was just thinking about you. You working? How's it going?" She gazed eagerly into the phone's camera.

"It's going." He tried to muster some enthusiasm. "Yeah, I'm working."

"Anything interesting happen at the orchard today?" she asked with a fluff of her long, brown hair. Stacey was gorgeous—there were no two ways about it. She could also be temperamental if he set her off. He usually was careful about what he shared with her.

Seth hadn't called her back after his meeting with Gia, but he'd planned to speak with her tonight, anyway.

He thought about the rest of his day since he'd talked to her. The plan to host more events at the farm was interesting.

Meeting Gia was interesting. She'd been a pleasure to talk to. There was something about her that really lit up the room. But he certainly wasn't about to tell Stacey any of that or she'd get the wrong idea. "Nah, same old, same old. We're going to start hosting more events—weddings and parties and stuff—though. Met with the agency today to get the ball rolling on an anniversary party we'll be hosting in about a month."

"Oh, that's great! We've had so many weddings here this summer." She leaned back. "But I'm sure you knew that already."

Seth nodded. The Henderson Estates hosted weddings every weekend during the summer, with frequent dates throughout the rest of the year as well. Weddings were big business in Sonoma. "Yeah, that's what gave me the idea."

He'd worked at the Henderson Estates with Stacey for two years and dated her the second one. She was a lifeline to that world—his old life, his old friends. As much as he was glad to be back, he missed his buddies. He hadn't met many people here yet, really, at least no one he had much in common with anymore.

His old high school friends had largely moved on—to the cities or the suburbs south of the peninsula or even out-of-state. Some, who were still local, had married and were having kids. Apart from a couple of guys he went to high school with who worked down on the docks, there was really no one to call up and meet for a beer on a Friday night, so he sometimes went alone and just watched a game on the bar's TV.

The Fourth of July a couple of weeks ago had been totally lame, if he were being honest. He'd stayed home and watched the fireworks from afar with his parents. Such a letdown.

He'd been too busy to try and have much of a social life, regardless. Most nights he was exhausted. The farm kept him busy. He'd had a lot of catching up to do on the books, the fields, the vines, and everything else. "So how's everyone doing?" he asked.

"Everyone's fine," Stacey replied. "You know how it goes around here in the summertime. Busy, busy. I miss you, though." She leaned into the camera and pouted.

"You too," he said, aware of how half-hearted he must sound.

"Is something wrong, Seth? You seem a little off."

"Nah, I'm fine." He shrugged.

"Okay. If you say so." Stacey changed the subject. "So I found a one-bedroom place that looks pretty good online. Do you think you could go and look at it for me in person? It's a month-to-month lease, and I'll have to send a month's rent plus security deposit if you think it's legit." She raised her shoulders with excitement and dropped them. "Only eight weeks until I leave. I can't wait."

Seth cleared his throat. "Uh, yeah, but I'm pretty busy this week. The festival's on Saturday. Send me the address and I'll see if I can find the time." His pulse quickened, but it wasn't with excitement.

"But I might lose it if I don't act on it quickly. What am I going to do if I can't find an apartment before I come out?"

Things with Stacey had been bothering him lately. It had been bad enough when he'd first left and they'd had to separate, having been forced into an unintended long-distance relationship. But he'd adjusted, and he figured it wasn't so bad, at least until they saw how things went for a while.

Which brought him to the question of how things were actually going, which weren't well.

He didn't really miss her anymore.

He'd gotten used to not having her around, and instead of longing to see her, he found that life was a lot easier without her. No more walking on eggshells because she wasn't having a good day. No more constantly feeding her endless need for attention. She did call and text a lot, but that wasn't so bad—she was easier to take in small doses.

In all honesty, he'd been having misgivings about their relationship for a few months before he'd even left California. Stacey was a handful. He didn't miss her tantrums.

And now this whole moving plan was starting to make him anxious. For someone who was from Wisconsin, to move back here seemed well, natural—easy. But for someone who'd never even been to the area before, who was just picking up her life and moving it all the way to Door County in the hopes that her relationship would work out—well, it was starting to freak him out.

But she was all in, willing to give up everything for him. He'd been with her for a whole year—so why wasn't he more committed? Why didn't he want this more?

Although he'd been able to push it out of his head and accept the plans they'd made until now, for some reason, tonight, he couldn't seem to get past the anxiety. He felt something growing in the pit of his stomach. It was too much.

"Hey, my mom's looking for me. I gotta go. I'll talk to you tomorrow, okay?"

Stacey sat back, her brows tight. "Uh, okay."

"Bye."

"Goodnight. I love—"

Seth ended the call.

He couldn't deal with it right now. He inhaled, staring out the window, and let out a heavy breath. He set the phone down and leaned back.

Stacey had attended Sonoma State and earned a degree in winery management, as well. He hadn't dated her until they'd been working at the Henderson Estates for a year, although they'd been acquainted all that time. They'd been a natural fit in many ways—similar interests, passions, and goals for the short term.

He played with the paperweight sitting on the desk and glanced at the laptop. How was he going to handle her moving here? Just the thought of it was making him squirm. This was nothing like when he'd dated her there.

In Sonoma, they'd been on equal turf. Both of them had gone to that particular region for their own reasons. But her only reason for coming *here* involved him.

What if she didn't like Wisconsin as much as she thought she would? And what if things between them didn't work out? What then?

He stared out the window for a few minutes at the evening sky, the setting sun giving a pinkish glow to the sky over the cherry trees. He tried to imagine their future together, but he couldn't seem to do it. He just couldn't picture her here. He wasn't sure he wanted to anymore, either.

How could he break it to her that her moving here didn't feel right to him? That he wasn't excited? Maybe he ought to suggest she visit first? But even that thought almost made him sick. What was the matter with him?

It was too much to think about. The festival needed to be his priority right now. He shook off the troubling thoughts and brought his focus back to the laptop.

THE WAITER LEFT with the check after dinner, and Gia walked to the parking lot with Tom and Kira. Outside, Nick pulled away in his Jeep, and Courtney waved from the front seat.

Kira turned to Tom and Gia. "I'll see you kids later."

"Adios, Nash." Tom had an affinity for last-name nicknames. "Hey, Gia, wait up a sec."

Gia stopped and turned around, switching her purse from one shoulder to the other. "Sure."

Tom walked over.

"What's up?"

"I'll walk you to your car."

"I'd love that." Gia smiled and put an arm through his.

They reached Gia's white Chevy Malibu and she unlocked it. Tom leaned against the driver's side door and took a deep breath. Gia leaned against the car next to him. Was something wrong? This wasn't the usual Tom.

He glanced off into the distance. "Hey, so I just wanted to say I know I joke around a lot, and you might not realize it when I say it..." He looked back at her. "But I'd really like to take you out sometime."

Gia's eyes shot wide. "Wow, uh..."

"I know this is out of the blue, and I don't mean to make you uncomfortable. I just—I just don't want it to go unsaid. I'd have to kick myself if I never got up the nerve to ask you seriously, especially now that you've met someone."

Gia shrugged, still startled. "Well, I wouldn't call him a *someone*. I mean, I just met him, and he hasn't asked me out. We're just working together." Not that she'd mind if he did ask her out, but that wasn't something she should really even be thinking about.

"Well, he should've, and he probably will. He'd be an idiot not to."

Gia recovered from the little shock and gently took his forearm. "Tom, that's so sweet of you. I appreciate your honesty. You know I think the world of you—"

Tom sighed loudly. "—Just not in that way?" He looked off into the distance.

Gia cast her gaze to the ground. "I didn't mean it like that." She looked back up at him and he met her gaze. "It's just that—we're friends, and I don't want to ruin that by dating you. I'm sorry, sweetie. I'm so sorry." The last thing she wanted to do was hurt him.

He sighed, his shoulders slumping. "That's what I thought—friend zone." He forced a smile. "It's okay. I had to give it a shot."

Gia wrapped her arms around his middle and squeezed. She heard him inhale the scent of the jasmine shampoo in her hair and she felt him return the squeeze. "Aw, honey, any girl would be lucky to have you. I mean, look at you." She pulled back and squeezed his bicep playfully. "You're gorgeous. You're smart. You're funny, and you're sweet. It's only a matter of time before someone swoops in and—"

"—I know, I know. Paints the town red." Tom sighed and pulled her in again. "You don't have to make me feel better."

"I wish things were different, but I—" Gia murmured.

"Shh...I get it." He held her tightly, his chin resting in the locks of her hair.

What a great guy he was. Tom was exactly the kind of nice guy she should be dating. But she just didn't get any butterflies with Tom. He was more like the big brother she'd always wanted.

"Okay. Thanks," Gia said. "I'm sorry, I just had to be honest with you." She adored Tom, just—like he said—not in that way.

"I know, and that's exactly why I like you. You're a good person. You deserve to be treated like it." He held her a little longer before he stepped back. "All right, well, you know where to find me if you change your mind, okay?"

Gia let out a breath. "Okay."

Tom opened the car door for her.

"Thanks."

"You betcha," he said dryly.

Gia gave him an apologetic look and slid inside. She turned on the engine then rolled down the window.

"If this guy breaks your heart, so help me..." He smiled.

"Don't even..." Gia cast him a wistful smile.

Tom laughed and waved as she backed out of the parking spot. "I'll talk to you soon."

She blew him a kiss. "Soon."

FIVE

Two evenings later, Seth pulled his father's red pickup truck into a sprawling apartment complex located about five minutes outside of Heritage Bay. Maybe if he saw the apartment, he might be able to imagine Stacey moving in there. Maybe things might start to feel more real for him. Maybe it would help.

He found the right building, parked, and shut the door to the truck. In a couple of minutes, a guy roughly his age pulled up in a golf cart.

"You here to see the one bedroom?"

Seth nodded. "Yeah."

"Nice to meet you." He climbed out of the cart and stuck out a hand to shake. "Tom Garcia."

"Thanks." Seth shook it. "Seth Pederson."

Tom hesitated for a moment, staring at him oddly, as if maybe they'd met before. Then he flipped a set of keys around until he found what he was looking for. "It's nice to meet you. Right this way."

Seth puzzled over the strange look and followed him up

a flight of stairs. The guy didn't look familiar. Should he know him? Maybe they went to high school together? Tom opened the door to the apartment at the top and flipped on the lights, and Seth followed him inside.

"So when would you need to move in? I have this unit and a few others just like it opening up next month. A few on the first floor, if you'd prefer."

"Oh, it's not for me."

Tom looked at him, confused. "Then who's it for?"

"For my, uh, my girlfriend. She's out of state right now."

"Oh, okay." Tom nodded, glancing back at him curiously. "Where's she live?"

"California."

Tom nodded slowly. "I see. Moving to Wisconsin? That's not something you see everyday."

"Yeah, I know." Seth nodded. Wasn't that the understatement of the year? "She'll be here in September, probably around the fifth."

Tom nodded again. "Okay. Well, we can prorate it to the day she moves in if there's no one on the waiting list for the unit. But if there is, she'll either have to pay the full month's rent or risk losing it. But September's usually not a problem. Most of the summer renters are out of here by the last day of August."

Seth nodded. "Right." He glanced into the bedroom and bath. Already furnished. Perfectly adequate. The kitchen and living area were nice, too. But the whole thing wasn't sitting well with him. He had to get out of there. He couldn't imagine Stacey living there—right there, in Heritage Bay—and the fact that it was becoming all too real was backfiring for him rather than reassuring him. "Okay, no problem. I'll have her get back to you," he said quickly.

"Sounds good. I'll have the office keep an eye out for her application. What's her name?"

"Stacey Lochner."

Tom nodded.

"Okay. Thanks a lot, dude. I'll see you later." Seth managed a polite nod and headed out the door and down the stairs before Tom could finish locking the apartment.

Shouldn't he feel more positive about this? How was he going to go through with it? Stacey would be here in two months.

When she first suggested moving to Wisconsin for him, he'd thought it was a bad idea. He probably should've recognized that as a warning and acted on it. Instead, when Stacey pushed the issue, he'd gone along with it, wondering if maybe she were right—maybe it could work? Maybe it was exactly what they needed.

But they were from two very different worlds, and his world, he was certain, would come as a shock to her. She had grown up in Northern California and had never traveled further than the northwest. She had no idea what a truly cold winter was, nor what it was like to live in such a quiet, remote place, especially during the winter, with none of her friends or family around. It would just be him and his family.

She had no idea what she was getting herself into. The people were different; the lifestyle was drastically different. She would be leaving behind everything she knew and spending a lot of money to make it happen, too, and he wasn't even looking forward to her being here. The guilt was practically eating him alive.

He thought leaving Sonoma would allow him to clear his head, and maybe they could work things out. But it had only served to reinforce the notion that they probably weren't meant to be.

He took a deep breath and drove back into town. He'd stop and get the groceries his mother had requested while he was out, maybe take a short walk along the lake to clear his head.

He'd even offered Stacey a job working at his winery. There weren't going to be many other options, after all, especially since September meant the busy season was over. But having her work on the farm meant more isolation for her. And more one-on-one time for them. How would she meet any other people and establish a normal life that wasn't wholly dependent upon him?

He had too many questions. Maybe he was just getting cold feet because Stacey's impending move involved a much bigger commitment than he'd ever given a woman in his life. But if he were ready for that commitment, shouldn't it feel right? Shouldn't he feel just as eager as she did?

GIA STROLLED the produce section of the local food market on Wednesday after work with Tom on her mind. She was planning to throw together some salads that she could take to the office for lunch. She stopped to bag some carrots and peppers.

Their conversation the other night had taken her by surprise. All the flirting he always did—she'd thought it was just for fun. She had no idea he was genuinely interested in her. If things were different...maybe?

But they weren't. She couldn't force the feeling, and she didn't want to lead him on. Still, it was nice to hear that someone of his caliber cared.

Then again, looking at it that way was only taking advantage of his affection for her. She shouldn't give him the wrong impression if she didn't have feelings for him. It wasn't fair to him and it would just be plain selfish of her if she led him on.

She turned a corner and deposited a head of red-leaf lettuce into her cart, scolding herself, then looked up. Seth Pederson stood directly in front of her. "Seth—hey!"

"Hey Gia. Small world!"

Well, this was a pleasant surprise. "I'll say. How's it going?"

"Can't complain," he said, looking a bit flustered. "You?"

She nodded. "I'm good." Wow, he was just as handsome as she remembered. She scolded herself for the thought—again.

Seth clutched a loaf of wheat bread and a box of bran flakes, which caught Gia's eye. "Oh, these are for my dad. My mom's got him eating right, but he's not complaining." He grinned. "He's almost out of his bedtime snack." He held up the cereal.

Gia nodded. "Kudos to your mom."

He laughed then looked at the assortment of fresh vegetables in her cart. "Wow. My father's doctor would like you—a lot."

She blushed, glancing at her cart. "Just need to grab some dressing and a couple of other things. Are you headed that way?" She motioned to another part of the store.

"Actually I am. I'll join you." What luck.

She pushed the cart and they chatted about the weather and what had been going on with each of them for the past two days. A few minutes later, they went through the checkout line together.

"Let me carry some of those for you." Seth grabbed two of Gia's grocery bags along with his own.

"Thanks. That's very nice of you." What a gentleman. Seriously, what were the chances they'd run into each other? It was a small town, but not *that* small...

"No problem. Where's your car?"

"Oh, I'm just out in the lot." He was going to help her all the way to her car? Her eyes were drawn to the muscular tone of his arms, and she turned her head away.

A minute later, he closed the trunk. "All set." He hesitated for a moment. "Hey, I'm glad I ran into you because I've thinking about some ways to advertise the winery regarding events, and I was going to call you about it. But since we're here, do you have a few minutes right now? I was gonna walk down to the docks and check out the lake for a few minutes. I've barely seen it since I've been home. You want to join me?"

Gia's heart skipped a beat. Her plans only consisted of streaming something on television that night, anyway, and Noreen would love it if she could find a way to drum up more business that might benefit them both. "Sure, that sounds great. I'd love to hear what you're thinking."

Seth smiled, still holding his grocery bag. "Okay, perfect."

"So where's your car?" Gia asked, locking hers.

"Just down the street." He gestured in the direction they'd go ,and she fell in beside him. They stopped at the truck to drop off the bag, and Gia realized that Tom had all but vanished from her thoughts. Being around Seth had a way of making her forget about everything else.

"By the way, you should've seen the look on Noreen's face when I told her about the barrel room," Gia said. "She was ecstatic."

"Really? That's great."

"So thank you for that. She's quite happy with me right now."

"You're most welcome, but I'll be she's always happy with you?" He winked at her and she couldn't hide her smile. *If only.*

He didn't need to know how much she had riding on the anniversary party—he had enough to worry about.

Half an hour later, Seth and Gia still sat on a bench at the marina, watching the sun as it teased the horizon over the shimmering blue of the lake. Fishing boats and speedboats bobbed on their moorings. The gentle sound of water lapping against the dock's footings had lulled her into a quiet, peaceful state.

They'd discussed Seth's ideas to advertise locally, and Gia offered to help him with some ad copy. She'd also suggested he list the orchard and winery on some wedding guide websites that the agency regularly used to find interesting locations for their brides.

"That's a great idea. Come to think of it, the Henderson Estates was listed in go-to guides like that for Sonoma and Napa. Maybe we should set our listings to serve the whole state? We might be able to expand our reach quite a bit."

"That's a great idea. We frequently have brides coming from Michigan and other neighboring states, at least in the summer."

She loved his enthusiasm. Gia glanced at the lake and back. "Have you got an estimate for your advertising budget? The listings aren't too expensive, but starting out you'll have a bit of a commitment to make before you'll see any return on your investment."

"I don't yet. I've got to take a closer look at the books

and talk to my dad about it, but I realize it'll be a long-term project."

"Okay, good, but it should start to pay off fairly quickly."

"Right. I was also thinking that since the winery's heated, it could be a really nice setting further into the fall, maybe even the winter."

He definitely had the right idea. She was excited to help make it happen. "Christmastime weddings are very popular, but they can become tricky because the weather doesn't always cooperate up here, or so I've been told." She hadn't yet spent a winter in Door County, but it probably wasn't too different from Minnesota.

"Oh, that's true. Maybe I should just target the local regions in the winter then? For those tough enough to travel —and shorter distances." He grinned.

"I think that's smart, at least for the first year, to see how it goes."

Seth shook his head. "I don't know why I wasn't thinking about how harsh the winters are here. We did weddings all year long in Sonoma. Such great weather there. Guess I forgot."

Gia nodded. "So everything continued the same as usual throughout the year there?"

"Yeah. Summertime definitely was busier, but a lot of weekends were booked throughout the winter." Seth stared out at the water and she studied his face for a second. He looked lost in thought.

"What do you miss the most about California?"

He turned back to look at her. "Hmm. Funny you ask because I was just thinking about that today. Remember how I told you I miss the people? Well, I do, but actually, I think what I might miss more is the stability of the situation.

Things just ran smoothly, and we weren't faced with the question of whether or not we'd be able to stay open every time we looked at the books."

"Oh, I bet," Gia's eyes went wide. "Your orchard—it's all on your shoulders. That must be a heavy weight to carry around everyday."

He nodded. "Yeah. The winery business at Henderson was booming. It almost ran itself. I just had to implement a few changes when I started managing the place—none of which were rocket science, by the way—and then things did even better. I miss how easy it was. I didn't appreciate it enough."

Gia nodded. It was nice to see a guy willing to admit it when things weren't under control. It took a confident man to be comfortable with a situation like that.

"Sometimes I almost wish I could go back. Not literally —just to running a business that isn't half underwater." He laughed ironically. "As much as I love the farm, I had no idea how good I had it in Sonoma."

"I get that. It's hard to live in the moment." She shook her head.

"It is." Seth leaned back against the bench and scrubbed a hand across his chin. "Especially when your life is half-stuck in the past."

Gia returned her attention to the bay where a crew on a sailboat was laying anchor for the night.

Seth turned to watch the boat with her. "So what about you? Do you like living here? I know you said you've only been here since April, too."

"That's right, and yes, actually I love it. I've still got some good friends in Minneapolis, but I've made some great friends here. There's a lot going on every weekend—at least right now. I guess we'll see how things go this fall."

"Oh yeah? That's good to hear because I haven't met many locals yet since I've been back, apart from you." He turned to look at her and grinned. "This has been a nice change of scenery. Thanks for coming out here to talk."

Gia tilted her head. Again, how lucky was it that she ran into him? "It's my pleasure. I don't spend enough time enjoying the views here, either."

He smiled.

She wanted to know more about him. "What about your old high school friends? Are you in touch with any of them? Some of them must still live here."

Seth explained how only a few did and how their lives had just become too different from his.

"Well, I'm sure you'll meet more people—maybe when things aren't so busy on the farm?"

Seth nodded.

"You know, I've met a great group of girls *and* guys here—you'd like them all. You could come out with us sometime if you'd like?" Gia ventured. "We usually go for a drink or two on the weekends, sometimes a meal first. We all went to the beach last weekend."

"Oh yeah? That sounds like fun. Let me know next time, if you wouldn't mind me tagging along."

"Okay, for sure." She shook her head. "And don't feel like you'd be tagging along. Everyone's always bringing other friends around. The more the merrier."

He fixed his gaze on her. "Okay, cool, if you're sure. Thanks."

"Of course." Should she push the issue? Oh, heck, why not? "We'll probably be getting together this Friday night, actually. Are you busy?"

"Hmm, unfortunately, this is the one Friday night that I really can't go out. We're having our annual cherry festival this weekend at the orchard—all day Saturday— and I'll be up with the rooster, as they say on the farm. It's been keeping me *very* busy lately."

She laughed. "Oh, that's right. You mentioned it the other day when we were discussing your event calendar. So what goes on at a cherry festival?"

He chuckled. "Oh, you know, a little of this, a little of that. You'd love it."

She laughed. Was he flirting? It was hard to tell.

"I'm just kidding, but it's a lot of fun. There'll be carnival games and lots of good food, and cherries to pick if you like to climb ladders." He grinned. "You should bring some of those friends and come on out for a few hours."

"Really? That sounds like fun." She would love to check it out. Maybe some of the girls would go with her? "And wow, a farm to run and now a festival? You really do have a lot on your plate." She was impressed.

He nodded. "This is our biggest public event of the year. Kicks off the real harvest, which starts next week after the festival."

"Exciting."

The sky was fading from a beautiful, hazy blue into a shade of purplish pink. A pair of gulls soared across the sky. "It's beautiful out here, isn't it?" she said.

"It really is." He turned his head and she felt his eyes on her. She smiled back then returned her attention to the lake, and they watched as the sun disappeared below the horizon.

"Well, I'd better get going. I'll be up with the rooster tomorrow, too." Seth grinned and stood up. "Busy week."

"Yeah, I'd better get home, too."

They walked back to Gia's car, and Seth waited while she unlocked the door. "Hey, so thanks for hanging out. I'm looking forward to getting the advertising started."

"So am I." Gia climbed into the seat. "And I'll send you links to those listing guides tomorrow."

"Thanks! I'll talk to you soon." He nodded and she backed out of the parking spot. If she weren't careful, she might start thinking about him as more than a business partner—maybe as an actual friend.

She smiled and settled into the seat.

That wouldn't be so bad, would it?

SIX

Seth reached his truck and heard his phone buzz with a message. He climbed into the truck and pulled the phone out.

It was a photo and a text from Stacey. She was smiling, standing arm-in-arm with a handful of the other employees at the Henderson Estates. The rolling hills of the vineyard gleamed in the background. The beautiful villa that served as the tasting room and restaurant were behind them. His old friends—fellow employees, guys and girls—their sunglasses blocking that never-failing California sun from their eyes.

Stacey looked pretty, the wind blowing her long hair away from her face.

Thought you wouldn't mind seeing everyone. We all miss you. xoxo

Seth stopped and stared at it. Something felt a little different from the last time she'd sent a photo like this. No pang in his chest for how much he missed that life. No actual sadness. And no sweeping anticipation for when Stacey would arrive in Wisconsin so they could restart their lives together. Instead, it felt a little more like dread.

Things were never going to be the same again. These people were quickly becoming a part of his past. He texted her back.

Thanks. Tell everyone I said hi.

A neutral reply was easier than none at all, when it came to Stacey. He started up the truck. The life he'd left behind had been great, but maybe this new life could be good, too.

SETH WAS UP BEFORE DAWN. Saturday morning had arrived, and there was plenty to do to get ready for the festival. He sucked down the last few drops of his coffee and skipped down the stairs of the old farmhouse porch. The early morning air was brisk, and the sky barely revealed the daylight. Vendors and trucks had begun to arrive with light equipment, and some of them were already setting up tents and booths on the property.

Seth walked the grounds, inspecting the progress. Everything seemed to be running smoothly. He checked his watch. Right on schedule.

Farmhands were taking stepladders, buckets, crates, and signage out to the fields, perching the ladders among the trees. Two employees were helping to decorate and prep the place for the crowds. He'd been pleased with the employees at the farm since he'd arrived. His father had really built a strong foundation for the business.

Seth's mom was rallying from warehouse to lawn to the big white tents, followed by two other employees rolling dollies full of jarred fruit preserves, dried cherries, baking mixes, mustards, and sauces from the market. Two local bakeries provided fresh pastries each year, and their trucks were unloading several hundred boxes of tart cherry pies and other assorted treats to sell under the tents.

Excellent. Now if the whole day could run this smoothly, they'd be in great shape.

Seth's father was outside, too, with a mug of decaf in his hand, directing some of the action from a lawn chair near the farm store.

His father had been warned outright by his mother that the last thing they needed today was another medical emergency, so he'd better take it easy and let everyone else do the heavy lifting. His father had begrudgingly agreed.

Seth hadn't been home for one of these festivals in years, but he remembered them well from his eighteen years on the farm. It was all-hands-on-deck on festival day, and he'd been looking forward to it for a lot of reasons, not the least of which that if everything went well today, they might even see a profit.

He exchanged a few words with the truck drivers, signed some order forms, and started in on a stack of chairs.

THE TANTALIZING SMELL of burgers and sausages on the grill came from a food truck parked next to the lawn at the Pederson Orchard, and a folksy band played a familiar tune on the banjo. Gia crossed the parking lot and meandered around the hedges and flowers. Several hundred people still milled about at the cherry festival.

She glanced at the time on her phone. It was just about five o'clock in the evening, and she was late meeting her friends. Noreen had called Gia this afternoon when she was on her way out the door, asking her to go to the office to discuss a last-minute booking for a wedding. The couple was interested in getting married at a winery in early October and they had some time to meet and go over their plans. They'd settled on a vineyard in Michigan, but the venue had fallen through. Fed up with the DIY approach, they now wanted someone to help plan the affair.

Gia had jumped at the chance and met with them, successfully securing them as a client. Now all she had to do was convince them to use the Pederson Cherry Orchard and Winery.

Why had Noreen put her on the job rather than Tara or Jackie? Perhaps it was because Gia already had the most information on this venue and had been the one to sell Seth on the idea of hosting more weddings on the property in the first place—not that she'd had any convincing to do. Whatever the case, it seemed like the only fair way for Noreen to handle it.

So it seemed Noreen hadn't lost *all* faith in her when it came to weddings. *Whew*.

Gia walked onto the festival lawn and glanced around at the booths and games. There were a few hundred people milling about. Where would Kira and Courtney be?

She stopped for a second in front of a tent shading tables full of countryside-themed décor when she heard Kira. "Hey, Gia! Over here!"

Gia smiled and joined them. "Hi, girls! How's it going?"

Kira gave her a quick hug.

"Sorry I'm so late."

"No worries. But our apologies, too, my dear—we both had a slice of cherry pie without you."

"It was really *the thing* to do here. We couldn't resist." Courtney gave her a hug.

"And it was out of this world." Kira rolled her eyes with pleasure.

Gia laughed. "No problem. I'll have a piece later, but I'm sorry I missed hanging out with you guys." She smoothed her strappy yellow tank top and stuck a hand in the back pocket of her jean shorts. "Thanks for coming. Did you have fun?"

"Yeah, it was a really nice change of pace," Courtney said. "I love coming out to the countryside, and the orchard is gorgeous. We played some of the games and walked around and watched people pick the cherries off the trees for a while. Kira took pictures. So how'd your meeting go?"

"It actually went really well," Gia said enthusiastically. "They want to come and see the facility this week. Hopefully, they'll like it. I can't wait to tell Seth."

"Oh, cool! Congrats!"

"Thanks!"

Kira glanced around. "So where do you think he is, anyway?" She arched an eyebrow. "The hot farmer who runs the place?"

Gia made a face at Kira and laughed, then scanned the crowd. She was a little nervous about seeing him. "Shucks. I don't know. He must be busy." The festival looked as though it had been a success. She wanted to congratulate him.

Courtney turned and glanced behind her. "We've been playing a game trying to guess who he is all day, but I don't think we found the right guy."

"You guys are funny." Gia glanced around. But where

would he be? What if she didn't find him? That would be a bummer.

"Well, I'll walk you to your car." Gia said. "I know you guys have to bail."

Courtney had plans with Nick tonight, and Kira was supposed to have dinner with a friend in Anderson Cove.

"Okay, sounds good," Courtney said.

Gia started toward the lot with them when she heard a familiar voice.

"Hey, Gia!"

Her heart skipped a beat, and she turned around. It was a good thing she was wearing sunglasses because her eyes went wide at the sight of him. The white T shirt he wore with his blue denims did nothing to hide the outline of his perfectly toned arms. She felt her cheeks flushing. "Seth! Hi."

Courtney whispered, impressed. "Nope, we haven't seen *this* guy yet... By the way, I'm so impressed, Gia."

Gia squeezed Courtney's wrist and shushed her, grinning.

He reached the three of them. "I'm so glad you made it."

"Me, too! It's great to see you." His smile was incredible. It was great to see him. She turned to the girls. "These are my friends, Courtney and Kira."

"Nice to meet you both," he said graciously. "Thanks for coming out today."

"So—great turnout, right?" Gia ventured. "It seems to be going well?"

"Yeah, it's been good. Nice and busy. Everyone's happy."

Gia removed her sunglasses, squinting toward the small corral that had been set up on the other side of the parking lot. "Has the line to the pony rides been nonstop all day?"

Kira nodded. "It has since we got here."

Seth glanced over at the corral. "Ponies are always a big hit with the kids."

"That's for sure."

Out of nowhere, Gia heard a clattering, and they all turned to look.

Seth winced and looked over his shoulder. "Uh-oh. Looks like one of the signs."

"And a lot of buckets," Kira added.

"Oh, no." Gia crinkled her nose.

"Well, hey, I'd better go take care of it. How long are you staying? This goes on until seven." He looked at his watch. "It's a little after five now."

"Actually, Kira and Courtney have been here a while and they have to go, but I just got here. I was called in to work earlier." She wanted to tell him about the potential booking but it wasn't the right time—he was in a hurry. "I was going to walk them to their car and then come back and take a look around."

"Oh, okay, cool." He looked at Gia. "Well, come and find me when you get back. I need to go check on the produce and baked goods tents after I deal with the mess." He pointed to it. "It's over there."

"Okay, sure." Gia stuck a hand in the front pocket of her shorts.

Seth glanced back at the overturned buckets. "I'm sorry I didn't get to show you all around a bit, but I'd better get going."

Kira grinned. "Oh, it's no problem. We had fun today."

Courtney nodded.

"I'm glad you liked it, and it was a pleasure meeting you, ladies."

"Likewise." Courtney replied.

He gave them all a friendly nod and skirted off.

Courtney and Kira turned to stare at Gia after he was gone, but neither spoke for a beat.

Gia looked innocent. "What?"

Courtney started in first. "Oh. My. Goodness. You've been holding out on us."

"What are you talking about?" Gia asked. "He's nice, right?"

"Yes, he is," said Kira. "But you didn't tell us he looks like a movie star!"

"Or that he's so charming!" Courtney chimed in. "And no, we definitely didn't see him earlier today. I would've remembered."

Gia giggled. "Shh. People might hear you."

Kira glanced around matter-of-factly but lowered her voice. "Don't worry, Stewart. No one can hear us."

"Seriously, he's really good-looking," Courtney whispered.

They started toward the parking lot.

Gia straightened her shoulders. "He is, isn't he? But I'm working with him. It doesn't matter what he looks like."

Kira turned to Gia. "We talked about this at dinner the other night. I still think it's fine. Plus, it's obvious he likes you."

"What? No. Do you think so?"

Courtney took off her sunglasses and grabbed Gia's wrist playfully. "He totally does. He asked you to come and find him. Guys don't talk like that unless they're into you."

Kira was stone-faced. "She's right."

"We're just friends." Still, it was an intriguing thought. Gia glanced in the direction Seth had gone. "I'll be honest— I really like him, but just as a person. I mean, he's sweet and thoughtful and smart."

Kira smiled. "Uh-huh. Now you're talkin'."

"But we have a professional relationship—and maybe a friendship." Could he ever be more? She had to admit it—she did find herself attracted to him, and that hadn't happened in a long time. Still, she had to be smart. Not only could it jeopardize her career, considering Noreen's current watchful eye, things could suddenly become very uncomfortable if she were to fall for him and he didn't reciprocate. She couldn't take that chance.

"But how often does a guy like this come along, seriously?" Kira reasoned.

She had a point. Good looks, brains, and a great personality—guys like Seth weren't easy to find.

Gia knew Courtney was a bit more reserved than Kira. "What do you think, Court?"

Courtney nodded. "I agree with Kira. I think it's fine. Maybe just keep it quiet in front of your coworkers. That's all."

If anything were to happen, she wouldn't let her coworkers—or her boss—know about it *at all*.

"Okay. Well, thanks, girls, but now you've got me all nervous!"

"That's the spirit." Kira grinned. They reached Kira's car and Kira unlocked it.

"Oh, don't be nervous, sweetie." Courtney patted Gia on the arm. "You've got nothing to worry about. Just give it a chance."

"We'll see." Now, if she could only wipe the dumb grin from her face.

SEVEN

A stack of cherry-picking buckets lay in a heap on the lawn next to an overturned U-Pick sign. Seth began to collect the buckets as a father marched his two young boys over to take responsibility for the mess. Seth shook the father's hand and helped the kids straighten up. He thanked the group, and the boys scampered off.

It had been great to see Gia and meet her friends. They seemed nice. It had finally become clear that moving back didn't have to mean the end of his social life, whether Stacey was in the picture or not.

Stacey.

She'd been texting him all day, even though she knew he'd be busy with the festival. Last night over the phone, he'd finally asked her if she wanted to visit before she firmed up a place to live, just to see if she liked it first. The apartment was going to cost a lot and he didn't want to see her lose any money over it.

She'd reluctantly agreed, but today, she needed reassurance that things between them were okay. Honestly, he wasn't sure, himself, but he literally had no time to spend on the phone with her today. There were more important matters at hand. The festival was beginning to wind down, but the lines of customers fanning out from the market tents were long. He needed to see how his mother and their employees were faring behind the counter.

He'd been pouring at the tasting room and checking on the various booths this afternoon. The last time he'd checked on his mother, she'd been somewhat busy. He slipped in under the tent and joined her behind the counter. Things had certainly picked up. He glanced around, encouraged. "Has it been like this for a while?"

"Yes, about an hour now." She handed a man his change. "I think everyone wants to get a little something before we close. It wasn't this busy this morning."

"You need a break, Mom? I can take over for a while."

She finished with the next transaction then stepped out of the way. "Sure. Thanks, honey." She promptly moved down to help at the next register, then sent their employee, Melissa, on a thirty-minute break and stepped into her place. Seth shook his head, grinning. His mother was tireless.

Seth got to work handling customers. About fifteen minutes later, he looked up from the credit-card reader to see Gia. "Oh, hey!"

She leaned in and kept her voice down. "Hey, it looks like you're really busy, so I'll probably just take off."

Seth tapped a few items on the screen, then handed the card back to the customer. He turned to Gia. "Are you in a hurry?" He didn't want to make her wait, but he wouldn't mind chatting with her when things slowed down a bit. It would be rude not to, anyway, since he'd asked her to come out today. "I'll be done here soon."

Gia nodded, glancing at the line. "No, not at all." She looked around. "But—do you want some help?"

He certainly wouldn't mind the help if it would make the line move more quickly.

He took two jars of preserves from a customer and rang them up. "That would be fantastic. You sure?"

"I'd be glad to," she said. "It's no problem."

"Okay, awesome. Come on back." He shot her a grateful look then turned his attention to the next customer. Gia stepped under the shade of the tent and set down her purse. Seth pointed to a stack of bakery boxes then rang up the purchase as Gia bagged a cherry pie and two scones for the customer.

In another five minutes, with the two of them working, the line was moving more quickly and growing shorter. She seemed to be a natural. Seth smiled at Gia. "Thanks. You're good at this."

Gia smiled.

Seth's mother returned, nodded politely at Gia, then walked over to Seth. A look of concern clouded her face and she spoke softly. "Honey, I don't want to worry you, but I have to run over to the house for a bit. It's your father. He didn't listen to me. I told him to take it easy, but..."

Seth turned away from the customers, wrinkling his brow. "What's wrong?"

"He says he's not feeling well. I'm sure he's fine, though." Her expression said otherwise.

"I'll go check on him."

"No, I'd rather go, myself," she insisted. "But Melissa's not due back for ten or fifteen more minutes. Do you think these people will mind if I shut down the line for a little while?"

Seth looked at her line. It was long. They couldn't

afford to turn away paying customers. "Oh, no, Mom, please don't do that." He glanced around to see if any other employees were near. "Hmmm. How about if..."

Seth's mother looked around anxiously, her phone in her hand.

Gia finished boxing some scones and handed them to a customer then approached Seth. "Is something wrong? Is there anything I can do to help?"

His mother blinked and sized up Gia. "I don't believe we've met." She looked at her son.

"Mom, this is Gia Stewart," Seth explained quickly, grabbing a cherry apple pie for his customer. "She's our event coordinator for the anniversary party. Gia, this is my mother, Clara."

His mother relaxed. "Oh, I see. It's nice to meet you, and I normally wouldn't ask such a big favor but I'm afraid we're in a tight spot right now. Can you work a cash register?"

"I sure can." Gia straightened her shoulders. "Worked at a grocery store during high school."

"All right, then, thank you!" his mother said. "Come with me and I'll show you. We'll have backup soon."

Gia hurried after her. About two minutes later, she came back to tell him that Gia was all set and hurried off toward the house.

Seth glanced over at Gia. She was already ringing up a few boxes of baking mix while chatting comfortably with a woman at the counter. It looked as though she'd been doing this all day. A smile crept across his face as he turned back to greet his next customer. Gia Stewart was full of surprises.

An hour later, Gia handed one of the last pints of fresh cherries on the table to a customer, and Seth rang it up.

Melissa had returned and resumed her spot behind the other cash register, but Gia had stayed to help.

Seth's mom had texted that his dad was doing better and that she'd put him to bed. It was just after seven and the line of customers had finally disappeared.

"That's the official end to another festival." Seth held a hand in the air. "Put it there, ladies. Great teamwork." Gia and Melissa gave him a high five.

"So should we start closing up shop, boss?" Melissa asked.

"Yeah, let's do it." Seth pulled out some crates from under the tables and started to clear the counters.

The day had gone smoothly, and judging from nothing more than the sheer number of customers he'd rung up in the past hour and half alone, it was likely they'd made good money today. He'd find out tomorrow morning when he went through the receipts. He was too drained to do it tonight. The only thing he could imagine doing for the rest of the night was relaxing.

Gia gathered up the last of the baked goods that hadn't sold while Melissa organized and boxed up the other merchandise. The equipment supplier arrived and began to break down all of the folding tables and chairs.

Seth emptied the cash and receipts from each register into a couple of zippered cases. He turned to Melissa. "I've got to take this to the safe and then see if things are under control everywhere else. You good with directing over here? Shawn and Trevor should be over soon with my truck to take everything that needs to go back to the warehouse."

"Not a problem." Melissa kept stacking.

"Great. Thanks." He'd finally get a chance to return Stacey's texts, but because of the time difference between them, she'd be busy at work for a few more hours. He'd send her a quick hello and tell her he'd call her later tonight.

He turned to Gia. "Okay, so I know you didn't plan on being here this long, but do you want to stay for a little while longer and help me celebrate the great turnout? Plus, I owe you a huge thank you for helping when you didn't have to." It wouldn't hurt to hang out and talk, right? He was allowed to make friends.

"It was no problem. I had fun!"

Seth waited. "But?"

"But sure, I'd be happy to stay." She looked even prettier when she smiled, if that was even possible.

"Okay, good. I just have to take care of a couple of things first."

Gia smiled. "No worries. I'll keep busy."

GIA LOOKED up as the last stack of boxed goods were loaded onto the bed of a pickup truck for easier transport back to the warehouse. The cleanup had gone quickly. Lending a hand was underrated. She'd had fun.

"Looks like you're just about done here?" Seth returned, and with a quick look around, loaded the dolly onto the truck.

Trevor nodded agreeably and hopped into the driver's seat. "Yeah, all set."

"All right, cool. Great job today, everyone! Thank you so much for all your hard work. I'll see you tomorrow."

Gia was impressed with the great relationship he seemed to have with his employees.

"Thanks, boss." Shawn waved, and they pulled away in the truck.

Gia gave Melissa a quick hug. "It was great to meet you. I'll see you around." Melissa left, and Gia turned to Seth. "Everything else under control?"

"Yeah, things are winding down. The guys should be all done soon. You ready to head out?"

"Yeah."

"All right, let's go." Seth tucked his phone into his back pocket and she fell in beside him. He let out a big sigh and raked a hand through his hair and across the back of his neck. "Wow, what a day."

Gia nodded. "This was quite an accomplishment. Are you happy with the way everything went?"

"Thanks. Yeah, very, but I'm even happier it's over." He winked.

Gia laughed and stuck her hands in her back pockets. "So where are we going to celebrate?"

"Actually, since it's such a nice night, what do you say we sit out behind the tasting room? At least until the mosquitoes eat us alive."

"That sounds great." Gia laughed and they headed toward the barn. The plan actually sounded fantastic, but she didn't want to seem too eager. "So how's your dad?"

"He's okay. He's sleeping now. My mom's asleep in the armchair, too. I peeked in at the house. Long day. It was a false alarm, I'd say."

"Your mom seems great, by the way."

"Thanks. She's one tough woman. This place would be in big trouble without her."

They reached the barn and found the doors still unlocked. A few employees were still tidying up. Seth said hello to them and went behind the bar where he grabbed a half empty bottle of red. "How's this?" He held it up.

"Perfect." A glass of wine really did sound like the perfect end to a pleasant evening.

He set it down then found a package of cheese squares in a small refrigerator and a box of water crackers from a lower cabinet.

"That looks good. I'm hungry." Gia was actually starving. She never did get that slice of cherry pie that Kira and Courtney had raved about.

"Me, too." Seth took two long-stemmed glasses down from a shelf behind the bar.

"One more thing." He reached below the counter and pulled out a candle in a wide ceramic holder, holding it up victoriously. "Citronella." He found some matches and stuck them in his pocket.

Gia grinned. "Worth its weight in gold around here."

"No kidding." Seth gave her a knowing look. "All right, let's head out back."

Gia took the candle from him and reached for the cheese and crackers. "I'll carry."

Seth grabbed the bottle of wine and the glasses, and she followed him outside to a seating area with a lovely view of the healthy side of the orchard.

He lit the citronella candle and they settled in at one of the decorative wrought iron tables. Seth poured two servings as the sun began to drop behind the orchard.

He handed a glass to Gia then took the other for himself. "Cheers to the close of another successful cherry festival."

"Cheers to that," she said with a wholehearted grin, clinking her glass with his. She took a sip. "Seriously, great job. This must've taken a lot of work."

"You have no idea." He laughed, took a sip, and pulled another chair in so he could rest his feet. "Honestly, I'm so glad it went well. I don't want my dad worrying about the place. The turnout should've eased his mind. I haven't looked at the numbers yet, but I've got a feeling we did well."

"Cheers to you, for doing such a great job. Seriously, this was a huge undertaking. Well done."

"Thanks." He nodded gratefully and took another sip of his wine. "Hey, thanks for helping out today. I really appreciate it."

"Oh, that's sweet, but it was nothing, and I honestly enjoyed it." She set down her glass and took a slice of cheese and a cracker. "Thanks for asking me to celebrate with you. I'm honored." She still hadn't told him about the potential booking.

He grinned. "It's just my way of paying you back for all the free labor."

Gia popped the snacks in her mouth and Seth grabbed some for himself.

She laughed. "Is it, now?" She snuck a peek at him. He was hardworking and determined, levelheaded, and a good leader—much more than just a handsome face. She pulled in another chair of her own and rested her sneakers on it. Tonight was turning out to be so much more than she'd thought it would.

"So listen, I have some good news. I wanted to tell you earlier, but we were too busy."

"Oh, yeah? What's up?" He peered across the table at her.

She sat up. "I've got a bride and a groom who want to come and see the winery this week. They're planning a small wedding for October—about one hundred people—and they're looking for a local winery. I met with them today—that's why I was so late. They hired us to plan their event. I think we can sell them on this place if you'll show them around."

"Really? That's great!" He sat up. "I'd be happy to show them around. What day were you thinking?"

Good! He was as excited as she was. "Probably Tuesday. Will that work?"

He gave a wholehearted nod. "Tuesday's great." He held up his glass again. "Okay, now we have to toast again."

Gia grinned.

"To the start of something great. You're amazing!"

Gia blushed and clinked glasses with him again. "Thank you!"

Why did it make her so happy when she made him smile?

A HALF-MOON SHONE in the cloudless sky, and the last of the festival trucks had left. The citronella candle still flickered in the darkness. All that could be heard on the farm now was the pleasant chirp of the crickets. Seth's glass was empty.

Two hours had flown by as he sat across the table from Gia. Two pleasant hours spent talking and laughing. Tonight had been his single most enjoyable night since he'd moved back three and a half months ago.

The conversation hadn't slowed for a second. Gia was easy to talk to and she seemed like she had her life together. She was ambitious and smart and independent. He admired that. She was also kind, helpful, nurturing, even.

What a contrast from Stacey. He felt guilty even thinking it, but even though Stacey was smart, passionate, and exciting, she was also needy and self-involved, on all but her best days. He rolled his eyes with a shake of his head and turned away from Gia. Not worth thinking about right now.

"What's wrong?" Gia asked.

"Oh, nothing." He played it off. "Just a lot on my mind." He glanced back at her and the shock of her long blonde hair pulled him in.

She was beautiful by candlelight. Or, by any light, for that matter. A pang of guilt crossed his chest and he looked away. He shouldn't be thinking about her like that.

It was bad enough that he couldn't seem to make a decision about his girlfriend, but it wasn't okay to have thoughts about someone else.

Gia looked over and smiled. "It's late. I'd better get going."

He checked his watch. It was after nine and he was exhausted, anyway. "All right. How'd it get to be nine already?" He stood up and pulled her into a standing position, meeting her gaze. "This was fun. Thanks for staying." Her hands felt soft and warm. He honestly didn't want to let go of them, but he dropped them quickly.

She tilted her head up at him and kept her gaze steady. "I'm so glad I did."

"No problem. Okay, let's get you safely on your way." He looked off into the distance and stuck his hands in his pockets. Why did he have the urge to grab her hand again? That wasn't something you did with a business associate or a friend. They'd become friends after all, hadn't they?

Still, he couldn't get the thought out of his head. What if he and Stacey were over and done with? He'd be free to ask Gia to go out with him. He'd be free to hold her hand the way he wanted to.

The parking lot was empty. He waited while she found

her keys and unlocked the car. Seth opened the door for her and she hesitated then slid inside and turned to look up at him.

Her face was almost wistful in the moonlight, like she didn't want to leave. He shut the door. Gia started the car and rolled down the window.

If only things were different.

"Thanks for a great night," she said. "And a great day."

"My pleasure. I'm so glad you came out for the festival."

"Me, too. Oh, and I'll see you Tuesday with the new client. I'll find out what time they're coming up and let you know."

"Okay, perfect. Good night. Drive safe."

"I will."

With a sadness he couldn't explain, Seth watched Gia pull of the lot and onto the main road.

He'd been standing in the dark for a few minutes when his phone buzzed from a back pocket, and the pit returned to his stomach. A text. It had to be from Stacey.

EIGHT

Seth headed back to the farmhouse in the dark. Stacey picked up on the third ring. Her text had asked if he was able to talk just then.

"Hey, how's it going?" he said casually.

"Great! I'm just having a few drinks, not that you'd care." She sounded like she'd already had one too many.

"What's that supposed to mean?" He switched the phone to the other ear but decided not to wait for an answer. She was probably still upset with him about asking her to visit Wisconsin before she made a decision about moving there. "I thought you were just getting off work?"

"No, they let a few of us out early today. It was slow for a Saturday and they overstaffed."

Sounded like the new management might be doing things differently. Overstaffing had never really been an issue when he was there. They were always too busy.

"Oh, so where are you?"

"At a bar downtown. I'm with Josh and Ty. A few of their friends met us here."

Josh and Tyler were younger guys who worked in the

tasting room at Henderson. They were known for their after-hour partying. Great. So she probably *was* drunk.

"So what have you been doing? Did the festival go this late?" She sounded suspicious.

"Nah. Just been hanging out, relaxing. It ended around seven. Everyone loaded up and left a little bit ago." It wasn't *untrue*.

She was quiet but he could hear talking and laughing in the background.

"Gonna be a late night?" he asked.

"Yeah, probably. Why didn't you call me earlier?"

"I'm sorry. I was just chillin' out. It was a long day. And don't you have to work tomorrow? It sounds like you've had a few."

"You're a little far away to be advising me on how late to stay out, don't you think?"

Oh no—here we go. Seth stopped walking so he wouldn't reach the house and wake up his parents.

He heard another voice in the background over the phone and Stacey laughed loudly at whatever was said. "I'll be right there, you guys. Wait for me!" She certainly had a pleasant voice for *them*.

"Stace—you there?" This was borderline ridiculous.

"I'm here. We're going to play some darts. I wanted Ty to count me in."

"So do you still want to talk tonight? Maybe I should let you go."

She huffed. "I don't know, Seth. There's not much to say. If you only want me to *visit* you, that kind of says it all. I might as well go have fun with some guys that want me around."

So she was definitely still mad.

Maybe he should come right out with it. "Look, I'm just

having my doubts about the whole thing, okay? I don't want you throwing your money away on an apartment here if you don't like it—is that so bad? I'm trying to save you some money."

"Gee, thanks." Her voice had an edge to it. "Is that all you're trying to do?" She was doing her best to make this difficult.

"What's *that* supposed to mean?" He knew what she meant—he just wasn't ready to talk about it right now, like this, but she was making him angry.

"That's supposed to mean you're trying to get rid of me. Don't try to deny it." She paused for a moment, and he heard the swishing sound of liquid from a bottle. He heard her swallow. She was acting as though it wasn't a big deal, but he knew it was just an act.

The truth was, he *had* been in denial about it lately, hoping she'd just change her mind, hoping the whole thing would just *not* happen. Confronting Stacey with his change of heart had been keeping him up at night. He didn't want her to come here anymore, but he'd failed to tell her. He'd failed to do anything. His indecision had brought things to a standstill. Why hadn't he just told her not to come at all? What was his problem?

Maybe this was his chance to be honest with himself and get the whole conversation over with. Except that she was drinking—which meant this wasn't the right time to have the discussion. It would be one hundred times worse if he broke up with her now. She'd throw a huge fit and end up screaming at him.

Still, the question remained: was he really ready to break up with her?

He sighed. Yes, he was.

"Listen, I don't want to do this right now. I've been up

since four a.m. I'm exhausted and I can't even think straight. Let's talk tomorrow. Go have fun with the guys."

"Sure, go ahead, blow me off. I obviously don't matter to you anymore, Seth." And there it was. Defensive, unreasonable, drunk Stacey.

"That's not it. It's just not the right time. You're out. Go play darts."

"The right time for what?" She paused. "Are you dumping me?"

She was baiting him. He didn't know how to answer that. He hesitated.

"You are, aren't you?" She swore at him. "I knew it. I knew this was coming."

"Stacey, calm down. Let's have a civil conversation tomorrow, okay? I'll call you then. Tell the guys I said hi."

He wasn't about to stand here and have her fire away at him all night. She couldn't be rational when she was like this.

"Goodnight, Stacey. I'll talk to you tomorrow."

"Don't hang up on me, Seth! Don't you dare hang up on me!"

"I'm not *hanging up* on you. I'm saying goodnight." Sometimes he thought he was dating a two-year-old, for crying out loud.

"Well, don't bother calling me tomorrow then! I'm going to make it easy on you. I'm breaking up with *you*!"

Seth stopped. Was she kidding? Guilt filtered over him —this could make things a whole lot easier on him. He was definitely *over* this whole thing, especially now. And why didn't he care? "*Are* you?"

"Yeah," she said. "How's *that* feel?"

Seth let out a heavy sigh. It felt like a huge weight off his shoulders, if he were being honest. "Fine, then," he said calmly. "We're done."

He heard her huff again. "That's it? That's all you're gonna say?"

It was his turn to get defensive. "What do you want me to say?"

"That I shouldn't do it—that you don't want me to break up with you! That we have too much history together."

"What?" This was really taking a strange turn. He snorted, shaking his head. "But you just said—"

"I know what I said!" She was yelling now. It was the booze.

"Look, we can talk more tomorrow. I've got to go. Really." His head was starting to pound.

She sounded angry, breathing heavily into the phone, but she finally went quiet. "Fine."

He heard a click and she was gone.

Seth shook his head and looked up at the sky, stretching out his shoulders. Could this be for real? Was it actually over?

All he'd have to do tomorrow, when she was calm, was tell her the truth, apologize, and be done with it. It was like a weight had been lifted from his shoulders.

THE NEXT MORNING, Gia jogged beside Courtney on a trail that meandered alongside the lake from Courtney's cottage.

"So how did things go with Seth yesterday?" Courtney ventured.

Gia glanced over at her, grinning. "Really well. I stayed and helped him out at one of the stands."

"Oh yeah?" Courtney grinned.

"Yeah. It was fun." Gia ignored the playful look. "Then we had a glass of wine on the barn's patio to celebrate the end of another festival."

"Oh really?" Courtney drew out the words.

Gia gave a nonchalant shrug as she ran. "Yes, *really*, but we're just friends. I mean—he hasn't made any moves and he hasn't asked me out on a date." Still, she thought she might've sensed something more when he'd looked at her last night. Whatever it was, he wasn't letting on about it. He probably didn't want to ruin their working relationship. She didn't either, but...

"Nick was like that at first," Courtney offered. That sounds very romantic, by the way—sitting outside at his winery."

Gia nodded. "It was, actually. But it wasn't like *that*." Although she'd wished it had been.

"So you don't get the feeling that he's interested?"

"I do, sometimes. But then he always pulls away like something's holding him back. I'm really not sure what's going on when he does that. He's very hard to read." Gia glanced at a sailboat cruising by on the lake.

"Does he ever call you?" Courtney asked between breaths.

Gia nodded again. "Only once, but it was about work."

"Okay, well maybe you ought to invite him out, but say it's for business. Maybe ask him to meet you for a business lunch."

"You think I should?" Honestly, she'd considered it already, but had decided against it so far.

"Totally. Oh hey—that reminds me, and this might be an even better idea: Jake's having a bonfire at his place next Friday. He's inviting a bunch of other people besides our usual group. He said to invite a few friends if we want. Why don't you invite Seth?"

Gia raised her brow and looked at Courtney out of the corner of the eye. That could be a way to turn this into more of a friendship rather than just a professional relationship, or possibly even more. And he had mentioned he'd like to meet more of her friends, but she'd have to be careful how she did it. She still wasn't sure where the line was and what might be crossing it. "You think I should? Because I don't want it to sound like I'm asking him out on a date."

"No, it wouldn't have to sound like a date. It's a party—just a chance to meet some locals."

Actually, he'd probably love to go. Gia should stop worrying. "He did say he hasn't met many people here since he's been back, but that he'd like to."

"See? I bet he'll say yes. Just keep it casual. It'll be fun."

Courtney was right. Seth would appreciate the offer. It didn't have to *mean* anything. And even if it did become *something*, Seth seemed like the kind of guy who'd treat her right. He, like Tom, wasn't like most guys.

"All right. I'll do it."

"That's the spirit." Courtney gave Gia a quick pat on the back.

SETH GLANCED at the clock on the nightstand. Just past nine on Sunday evening. The day had been busy, putting away signage and props after the festival, cleaning up a little trash that had been overlooked, getting ready for the harvest, which would begin tomorrow, and going through the festival's receipts.

They'd made a decent profit. Seth was happy with it,

but he was tired. It had been a long week. He lay in bed with his head propped up on a stack of pillows. His parents had already gone to bed, but he'd been staring at the wall for who knew how long. He broke his gaze and picked up his phone.

It would only be seven o'clock on the West Coast. Stacey would be home from work by now. He'd texted her earlier, knowing she would be more reasonable today, and she said she could talk tonight. They usually talked around this time on Sunday nights anyway.

He'd thought about things all day. What a mess she'd been last night. But he shouldn't have been surprised. He'd been a jerk to her, not telling her what had been on his mind for so long. Stringing her along when he should've confronted his misgivings a long time ago. He'd been withdrawn from her for weeks.

And on top of that, their relationship hardly felt real to him anymore. Phone calls and video calls, texts, photos—they weren't enough to keep a relationship going, at least not for him. It was absurd he'd kept it up all this time. But the fact of the matter was that he'd even been lying to himself.

He clenched his jaw and ran a finger over Stacey's name on his phone.

Stacey picked up the video call after only one ring, guilt quickly registering on her face. "Hey, stranger."

"Hey," he said softly. Not surprisingly, she seemed a whole different person today.

He asked about her day and she answered in a few words, then he filled her in on the outcome of the festival when she asked. Finally, he sat up in the bed. "Stace, we need to talk."

Stacey went quiet for a second, her expression changing. "I know. I'm really sorry, babe. I got out of control last night. It's just that I miss you and all of this is messing with my head." Her face was full of longing. "I never meant to break up with you. I was just angry. Can you forgive me? Can we start over and pretend that it never happened?"

Oh, no. He hadn't seen that coming. Now he'd have to put her through it all over again.

He shut his eyes and pinched the bridge of his nose. Where should he start? He'd thought they'd be past this.

"Listen, I get it. You were upset with me. You had every right to be, but this isn't going to work."

"What's not going to work?" She looked confused.

Seth let out a heavy breath. "I, uh, I've been thinking about our situation a lot lately. You were right about me. I wasn't being honest with you, and I apologize for that. I should've told you how I was feeling. But I'm being honest now. I don't think you should move here."

"Well, I kind of figured that when you told me just to visit first. But why not?"

Seth gazed at her. "I just don't think it's a good idea. There are just too many unknowns."

"Unknowns? Like what? What are you talking about?"

"Like—if you'll even like it here. It's really, really different from what you're used to. And it practically shuts down here in the winter. Plus, it gets so cold."

Stacey waved it off. "I already know about the cold. I'll be fine. I'm looking forward to the snow."

Seth shook his head. "It's not just snow." She had no idea what she was getting into. Wisconsin was anything but *just snow*.

He stared into the camera. "And it's not just *that*."

"What is it, then?" She flinched slightly. "Look, I'm a big girl. I can handle change. I'm willing to do this for us."

"That's just it—I know you are. But my heart's not in it." Seth stopped. He put his hands on top of his head. This was even harder than he thought it would be. "I can't do this anymore, Stacey. This whole thing—it's not going to work. It's too much. I can't do it."

Could she understand? Would she?

Stacey persisted. "But—the visit, the apartment. I was planning to come and see it. I was going to buy a plane ticket this week." She shook her head. "You're just getting cold feet."

"No, I'm not. And I'm sorry." Seth shook his head gently. "Forget about the apartment."

"But..." Stacey began, then let the sentence drift off. Tears started to stream down her face. "So, then—okay, we can just keep going on like we have been, I guess? Is that what you're saying?"

"No, babe, I'm sorry, but I'm not willing to carry on a relationship from seven states away anymore. I thought maybe you understood that last night when you were angry enough to break up with me. This whole situation can't be making you happy, either."

"No, I didn't realize you were so sure about it. I thought maybe I was imagining things. I'm perfectly happy," she whined.

He frowned. She couldn't be telling the truth right now. "No, you weren't imagining things. This is really hard for me to say, but we aren't right for each other." He spoke more slowly. "I can see it, now that we've been apart all this time."

"What are you saying then?" Stacey held her breath.

"I'm saying that if you didn't mean it last night when you broke up with me, then I'm really sorry, and I should've been honest a lot sooner, but I'm afraid I'm breaking up with *you*."

Stacey sucked in a breath. A few moments passed in silence.

He hated to hurt her this way.

"But—we have so much together," she countered. "And you're not even giving it a chance." She wiped her eyes. She wasn't going to give up easily, was she?

Seth rubbed his temple. "I *have* given it a chance. I've been giving it a chance for almost three-and-a-half months now, and I'm really sorry." He looked at her more closely. "Are you okay?"

Stacey didn't answer. She burst into tears.

Seth took another deep breath. "I know we started out with our lives heading in the same direction when I was out there, but things are different now, and we both have to admit that. You knew I was always going to come back here and run this farm someday—it just happened sooner than we thought it would. And honestly, Stacey, I'm not the same person I was just a few months ago. This place, these responsibilities—they've already changed me." It was the truth.

"But that's why I want to move there, Seth, so I can be a part of that change. I'm willing to do that for you."

"But I don't want you to anymore," he sputtered. He lowered his voice. "I'm not willing, okay? You have your own life to live, your own choices to make. You shouldn't come here if you're only doing it to follow me—and that's what this would be. This place—it just doesn't fit you, Stace. I can't picture us living here, trying to make a life together. I just can't picture you here."

"Don't say that, Seth," she whimpered. "I love you."

"You're not listening to me, babe. Please, just hear me.

This has been eating away at me for a long time now." Seth paused. "It's over between us. It's just not meant to be. I'm sorry." He looked at the wall. It was hard to meet her gaze after all he'd just said. He wished he could put his arms around her and make her feel better, though—at least a little.

Stacey sniffled, wiping away the tears that streamed down her cheeks.

He looked at her again. "Take care of yourself. Okay?"

Stacey stared at him through the phone—her eyes red, her cheeks dripping. "Please, Seth, don't do this. I never meant to break up..."

He set his jaw and shook his head. "I'm sorry, Stacey. It's for the best. Goodbye."

Her eyes begged. "No."

"I'm sorry. I'm so sorry." With a blank stare, he ran his finger over the red dot on the screen, ending the call.

He set the phone down and closed his eyes, gripping his head in one hand. He sat there for a few minutes, not moving, then finally, lay his head back on the pillows.

She'd be all right once she calmed down, right? Something like this was hard for anyone to take. She just needed time. There were plenty of guys there who'd jump at the chance to take her out, once she was ready.

He rested his head on the pillow, a mess of emotions. This was the end of a big chapter in his life. As rocky as things had been between them at times—and wow, she'd put him through the wringer more than once—they'd been together a long time, and he'd hurt her tonight. He'd never intended to hurt her. Yet, it had to be done. Still, he felt sorry about it.

Even so, it was liberating to get this off his chest, and

already, he felt more optimistic about the future. He could finally start moving ahead with his life.

He checked the clock again. 9:45. The harvest was starting tomorrow. It would be an early morning.

He turned out the light. For the first time in a long time, he might actually get a decent night's rest.

NINE

The Jenkins Event-Planning Agency rented space in a lovely, historical two-story home situated in what had become the commercial district of Anderson Cove. The building had been repurposed into office space, and it was only a stone's throw from several charming shops and restaurants. Gia sat at her desk on Monday afternoon and read a text from her mother.

Her mother checked in on each of her three daughters about once every week. Gia's older sister lived near their parents in Minneapolis with her husband and young children, and Gia's younger sister was still away at college in Michigan. Her mother kept tabs on all of them and shared their news with each other if they hadn't found the time to chat, themselves. Gia loved hearing about what was going on with everyone, but right now wasn't the time. Noreen wasn't a fan of personal calls at the office unless it was on a lunch break. Gia tapped at the phone.

Doing fine, Mom, but I'll call you tonight. Have to get back to work.

The bride with the October wedding had called. Gia swiped over to Seth's number and let it ring.

He picked up. "Gia. This is a pleasant surprise. How are you?" It was great to hear his voice.

"Good. Thanks! Yourself?" She shared a spacious workroom with Tara and Jackie, each with a sectional desk, and each within earshot. Better not sound *too* excited to talk to a client or a vendor or they might wonder what was up.

"Good," Seth said. "I'm taking a quick lunch break at the house. The cherry harvest started today so it's been busy around here."

Seth had explained the other night that on Monday morning the tractors and heavy equipment would arrive at the orchard to start the industrialized process of shaking the rest of the cherries off of the trees. Even after the U-Pick on Saturday, there would still be a good amount of fruit left to harvest.

"Oh, yeah? How's it going?"

"These guys know what they're doing. I'm basically just standing back and watching. It shouldn't take as long this year since only a third of the orchard has any significant fruit, anyway."

"Oh right. Well, that's great." Gia crossed her legs. "So hey, that couple who'd like to tour the winery tomorrow is hoping to be there around noon. Would that work for you?"

"Sure, that's perfect." He sounded more relaxed than usual. He must be doing better now that the stress of the festival was behind him.

"Okay, great. So how'd the business do with the festival? I'm guessing you've gone through the numbers by now?"

"Yes, I actually did, and they were good! I'm very happy with it. Thanks for asking."

"That's great! I'm so happy to hear that. So we'll see you tomorrow. Oh, and Noreen finished the paperwork for you. I'll bring it with me."

"Okay, great. Looking forward to it. Just text me when you get here and I'll come out."

Gia hung up and set her phone on the desk. She couldn't wait to see him, and what a relief the festival had done well. Seth deserved a break. She returned her attention to an open document on her computer. She'd have to invite him to the bonfire when she saw him tomorrow. Jackie and Tara would overhear if she mentioned it now.

IT WAS REFRESHING to receive a text without the follow-up sense of dread or anxiety. Midday Tuesday, Seth sat in his office going through the payroll numbers when his phone buzzed. It was Gia—she was outside with the bride-and-groom-to-be. He headed out.

After the introductions were made, they all shook hands and Seth gave the young couple a short rundown on the property. He actually loved this part of the job—talking to people and sharing what he thought he could do to serve their needs and make them happy. His mother always swore he'd been born a salesman.

If signing up brides and grooms got to be a regular thing, Gia could use his sales pitch and take people around by herself so he wouldn't have to be here every time, but for the first few clients, he wanted to be a part of things.

They walked the grounds, and he showed them the patio and the lawn with the arbor. The bride agreed that holding an outdoor wedding was not a great idea in October in that part of the world, because as beautiful as the setting was, it could be too chilly or it could rain. But they loved the look of the red barn and silo for their big day.

Gia started in on suggestions after they'd entered the facility. "So what if you did the ceremony here in the tasting room?" She mapped it out by walking the area, gesturing where the aisle and the altar could be. Seth watched as the bride's face lit up.

Gia led them into the barrel room. "And then, what if you did the reception in here? There's room for everything with the size of your guest list." She went through some possible placements for a dance floor and the tables.

The bride nodded but looked uncertain. "It's very intimate."

That was usually code for *too small*. Seth nodded. "The catering company could probably turn the tasting room back into a bar and lounge for your reception after the ceremony is over, too, so your guests would have more room to mingle."

"Right, that's an excellent point," Gia said. "I'm sure it could be turned back into a lounge once everyone's seated at the dining tables. And actually, if we could start much earlier in the day you'd have more hours of daylight? Maybe around one or two p.m. Would that be possible, Seth?" He nodded.

"Not a problem. We can close the tasting room entirely that day—it's not an extremely busy time of year for wine tasting guests around here, anyway. Oh, and you'd have full access to the entire barn and the grounds while your event is going on. The orchard store stays open until five on Saturdays but the parking lot's never crowded in the fall."

"Okay, that's great. Do you like it, honey?" The young bride waited for her fiancé to respond.

"I like it, but whatever you think." It looked like, at least, he'd be easy to convince.

"Oh, and you'd have access to the outdoor patio, too, but making use of it would depend upon the weather, of course," Gia continued.

The woman nodded. "Is there any sort of facility that could function as a bridal room—you know, like where I'd get ready and sort of *hide out* before the ceremony so no one else can see me but my bridesmaids and my parents?"

Gia looked over at Seth.

Hmm. That hadn't occurred to him. "Well, we have nice restrooms inside the barn with a small powder room—you can check them out before we leave." He pointed. "But a bridal room, per se..."

Gia jumped in. "In a venue like this, where there isn't a dedicated bridal room, the bride and bridesmaids often gather at the bride's hotel room for an hour or two, and then come over in a limo. The restrooms located over at the store building are accessible from the outside, however, so we could technically set those up as a place for you to hide out and take care of any last minute hair or makeup emergencies."

The bride smiled. "Perfect."

Close call. Good save, Gia.

"And the groom and groomsmen would do the same at the hotel." She turned to address the groom. "We'd get you your own limo."

He nodded agreeably.

"And where would the caterers work?" the bride asked. "I don't see any kitchen facilities."

Gia looked around and glanced at Seth.

"You're right. There's no kitchen here, but there's one in the warehouse where we do our canning. But they'd set up tents outside, just like they do for the outdoor weddings, and we can offer them hookups to the running water in the warehouse. And there's a sink behind the bar in the tasting room, of course."

The groom looked satisfied.

"There's plenty of room out back by the warehouse for the tents. Your guests wouldn't even notice them."

Gia shot him a grateful look.

"Okay, well, I absolutely love it!" The bride seemed to have had her questions answered. "Oh, but wait—what about photos? Can you show me some outdoor spots where we could do the group photos?"

"Absolutely." That was an easy question. "Follow me."

He led them out to the patio and walked to the edge where the orchard stood in the background. "Your date is, what—October seventh?"

"Yes, the seventh," the bride answered eagerly.

That was a perfect time of year there, before the autumn storms started coming in. "At that time, generally, most of the leaves are still on the cherry trees with lots of fall color, so this will still be a beautiful backdrop for photos, as long as it's not raining."

The bride looked impressed. "Oh, I'll bet it's beautiful. I've always wanted a countryside fall wedding."

Gia smiled at Seth and he caught her eye.

"And if it is raining," Gia chimed in, "we can use the barrel room and the ceremony area for photos." She pointed to the tasting room. "We'd have to just put a contingency plan in place to start much earlier and do all the group photos before the wedding. We'd be able to firm up the plan the week before the wedding, when the weather forecast becomes available."

"I like that idea, regardless. I don't want to have to miss

too much of my reception to take photos. Except for the ones right after the ceremony when we're first married." She smiled sweetly at her groom.

It seemed like Gia might be sealing the deal.

"Absolutely. I'll make a note of it." Gia tapped some notes into her phone.

"The whole peninsula is a popular destination for folks looking for fall foliage, actually," Seth said. "You could mention that in your inserts—when you send out your invitations."

Seth had worked enough weddings at the Henderson Estates to know how these things worked. Families were often looking for other ways to entice their guests to spend the money to attend a faraway wedding and offer them more of a destination for their overnight stays—things to do and places to see. Door County had plenty of that in the fall.

"That's a great idea. Your parents would love that," the groom said to his bride.

"So would yours," she replied, grabbing his hand. She turned to Seth. "Would it be okay if we took a look around outside on our own for a little while?"

"Absolutely. Have at it. We'll wait in here."

"Take your time," Gia said. "I want you to be perfectly sure."

A few minutes passed as the couple explored the grounds.

She turned to Seth when they were gone and brought her voice down to a whisper. "I think we've got them, don't you?"

Seth nodded. "I think they're hooked. We just need to reel them in." He motioned like he was casting a fishing rod.

"By the way, did you remember to bring the contract? In case they want to sign?"

"Yes, I have it right here. Fingers crossed." She held up a folder. "I've already talked with them about what it would cost to rent the space, so no need to bring any of that up." He'd given her the figures last week. Events like this would make a decent profit for him. He was more than eager to make the sale today.

"Okay, great. Thanks for the heads up."

A few minutes later, the couple returned, full of smiles, and said they wanted to sign on the dotted line and reserve the date. The bride snapped some pictures of the various spaces inside the tasting room for future reference and Gia took a picture of them outside the barn together.

Seth and Gia saw them to their car.

"We'll talk soon," Gia said. "Thank you so much. It's going to be great!"

They pulled away, all smiles.

She had done it—she had brought in his first wedding clients. The farm was headed in the right direction. What couldn't this woman do?

She turned to him, her face full of glee, her shoulders high. "We did it!" She looked as excited as he felt.

"That was great work!" He couldn't help himself. He reached out and pulled her in for a congratulatory bear hug.

She felt soft and warm and she smelled sweet, like jasmine and vanilla. She hugged him back tightly and he held her a moment longer than he probably should've.

He released her and she stood back, still smiling big. "Thanks! But you were just as good! And you saved me a few times."

"I think we actually made a pretty good team." Seth held up his hand and she slapped it in a high-five.

"I think you're right," she said.

"Seriously, that was great. And I think it's really going to be beautiful, especially hearing you describe where stuff could go and how you'd make it all come together. You're amazing."

He meant it—she really was. He gazed down at her and felt the urge to grab her hand again, the same way he'd wanted to the other night, but he ignored it, of course. This was no place for that kind of behavior. They were working together, and he shouldn't cross that line. She probably wasn't looking for him to hit on her, anyway.

Besides, he'd literally just broken up with his long-term girlfriend two nights ago.

Gia nodded vigorously. "Thanks. It's going to be gorgeous. And it was my pleasure." She took a few steps toward her car. "I should get back to the office."

"I'll walk you." Seth followed her.

"Hey, so I wanted to ask you something else while I have the chance." Gia started.

"Oh yeah, what's that?"

"A friend of mine is having a bonfire at his place on Friday night. It's a party—but nothing major. Are you busy? I thought you might like to meet some more locals."

Wow, he hadn't expected that. "No, I'm not busy." He grinned. Maybe his new life here *could* begin already. "I'd love to come."

TEN

Gia pulled out of the orchard's lot. She couldn't believe it—just like that—she had another wedding account to handle, despite the mishaps of the last one. She'd managed to land this one all by herself, too—well, certainly with Seth's help, but no one else, apart from Noreen giving her the chance with the couple in the first place. Which, of course, was huge. Noreen was going to be thrilled.

Gia would do her very best and prove herself. She'd come too far to drop the ball again.

And Seth was right—they'd made a great team. She was looking forward to working on the wedding with him, and others, if she were lucky.

Who was she kidding? She felt like the luckiest girl alive right now.

And he'd be coming to the bonfire! Her jaw was actually starting to hurt from all the smiling.

SETH DROVE his red pickup truck down Highway 42. A couple of turns brought him to the right street, where he slowed down to check the numbers. When he found the address, he turned and headed down a long driveway onto the property. A small cabin stood at the end inside a wooded area. He checked the time on the dashboard: 8:30 p.m. Gia said she'd be there by then. He scanned the driveway and recognized her car.

No one had ever accused him of being shy, but it was still a little unnerving to walk into an unfamiliar setting among a group of strangers—most of them—who probably all knew each other. Still, it was now or never. He got out of the truck, grabbed the six-pack he'd brought, slammed the door shut, and headed up the stairs. He gave a gentle knock to the door.

A slender, attractive young woman in denim shorts with jet-black long hair opened it. "Hi there!" she said.

"Hi, I'm Seth. Gia invited me."

"Of course. Come on in. I'll take you around back. She's outside, I think. I'm Angela." Angela motioned for Seth to follow and led him through the cabin's snug but comfortable living room.

"Thanks." He followed her into the kitchen and out onto the back porch. Outside, a large, grassy back yard was surrounded by cedar, hemlock, and sugar maples common to the area. Seth recognized a song from the indie charts playing softly from a set of speakers on the porch.

It wasn't dark yet, but a fire burned low out in the yard. About a dozen people sat around the fire chatting on backless wooden benches made from split logs and tree stumps. A few others stood around the yard chatting and sipping from drinks. It was an inviting scene.

Angela called from the porch. "Oh, Gia!"

Gia turned and smiled when she saw him.

"I've got something in the blender," Angela said. "Talk to you guys in a bit."

"Thanks. No problem." Seth descended the short staircase.

Gia strolled over, hands in the pockets of her jeans. "Hi! I'm so glad you made it!"

Seth flashed a smile. "Me, too."

She looked cute in a pair of jeans and a crop top with sandals, her blonde hair falling softly across her shoulders.

"Did you find the place all right?"

"Yeah, it was no problem. I had some friends that used to live over here when I was growing up."

Gia nodded. "Oh, good. And I see you came prepared?"

"Absolutely." Seth held out the craft beer he'd brought. "Would you like one?"

"Sure, thanks," Gia took a bottle and he used an opener on his keychain to pry off the lid.

She looked at the label. "This brewery is right near my old apartment in Milwaukee."

"No way? I love their stuff."

"Me too." She took a sip. "Thanks."

Seth looked at the yard and the house again as he opened a bottle for himself. "Nice place."

"Yeah, isn't it? It feels like you're totally out in the wilderness. He's got half an acre here. No neighbors close enough to mind a little noise."

Seth laughed. "I know how that is."

"Right, you would." She laughed.

"Hey, so, cheers," he said, clinking his bottle to hers. "Thanks for inviting me out."

Gia's smile was gorgeous and he found himself wanting to grab her hand and pull her close. But he stopped himself.

He didn't want to assume anything. He had no idea how she felt about him, and right now, he was just happy to be making some new friends in the area. *Don't go screwing things up already.* He looked away from her and glanced around the yard.

"Let's stash the rest of these on some ice," she said, turning.

"Sure." He followed her around the side of the porch where they found a cooler next to a stack of wood for the fire.

"Come on, I'll introduce you." Gia approached the firepit, found an empty bench and sat down. Seth followed her. "Hey guys, this is Seth."

Seth nodded and said hello then took a seat next to Gia.

"Hi, Seth," Kira said. "Great to see you again. Glad you could make it."

He grinned. "Thanks."

Courtney was sitting next to Kira and greeted him warmly. She introduced her boyfriend, Nick, who stood up and shook hands with him, then Gia introduced her friend, Jake, and then Marcy, who sat on the other side of the fire talking with a few people that Gia didn't know.

"Thanks for having me, man," he said to Jake.

Gia glanced at him. "Seth's local again after—how long were you gone?"

"Nine years. I left for college at eighteen and just moved back a few months ago."

"Wow. Welcome home, man," said Nick. What brings you back?"

Seth explained about the farm then gave them a quick rundown on his stay on the West Coast and his father's recent emergency.

"Heavy duty," said Kira.

Seth explained that his father was doing a lot better lately.

Seth turned to Jake. "Great place you've got here. How long have you had it?"

"Thanks." Jake nodded. "About two years. I love it."

Jake looked familiar somehow. "You said you grew up around here?" Seth asked.

Jake nodded.

"Whereabouts?"

Jake told him. "Wait—we went to high school together. You graduated a year ahead of me!"

Jake nodded enthusiastically. "I thought I recognized you from somewhere, dude. Welcome back!"

Jake and Seth caught up while Nick and the girls chatted. For a moment, Seth caught Gia smiling at him, and he winked at her. He liked her friends.

He took another sip of his beer. It felt good to be out. It had been too long.

Angela showed up with a few mixed drinks and handed one to Jake and one to Kira. "Blended, no salt."

"You're the best bartender around, Ang." Kira took a sip.

"I know." Angela cocked an eyebrow and sat down, clinking glasses with Kira.

Seth smiled. He liked this group.

'Thanks, Ang." Jake took a gulp and prodded at the fire with a metal rod. "Time for another log or two. If you'll all excuse me?" He handed the drink back to Angela. "Would you mind holding this for me for a sec?"

"Of course not." Angela grinned. "But don't be too long or I might have to drink it for you, too."

Jake grinned and stood up. "You do and I'll tackle you."

"Definitely drinking it, then." She smiled deviously and Jake laughed.

Seth laughed. "I'll help you, Jake."

Near the back of the cabin, another group of people stood talking as he and Jake walked over. One of the guys looked up and Seth did a double take. The guy glanced at him. "Hey, we've met somewhere, I think?"

The dude sized him up, looking a little surprised. "Oh, yeah. You looked at one of my apartments," he said coolly.

"Oh right." That was it. The apartment for Stacey.

"Tom." Tom held out his hand but seemed to be eyeing him cautiously.

"Right. Seth." Seth shook his hand.

Tom took a sip of his beer. "So are you a friend of Jake's?"

"Nah, we just met. Well, we went to high school together, as it turns out."

Tom nodded. "Oh. So how'd you end up here tonight?"

Tom's tone was still strange. Had Seth done something to offend him? "Through Gia. Do you know her?"

Tom furrowed his brow. "Yeah, I know her well."

Jake passed them clutching an armful of logs for the fire and cast a curious glance at the two of them. Tom shot Jake a look and Jake walked off. What was this about?

Tom's voice was a little louder. "So is your girlfriend still moving to town?"

Seth stopped, taken by surprise, and looked around to see if anyone else had heard. It didn't seem like anyone had.

"No, Stacey's not coming anymore."

"Oh, really, because she hasn't told us yet."

The truth was, he hadn't talked to her since their long talk on Sunday when they'd officially broken up. He just figured she would've let the apartment complex know she wasn't coming by now.

But what did this guy care?

"I'm sorry," Seth said, his tone sharp. "Have I done something to offend you?"

"I'm glad you asked. No—not yet," Tom said and turned and walked away.

Seth stood there. What just happened? He looked back at the group and saw Tom take Seth's seat next to Gia. Gia gave him a hug and he watched as Tom held her embrace.

Ah-ha. That made sense.

But there was nothing more than a friendship between himself and Gia. Why was this guy all worked up?

Seth grabbed a stack of logs, returned to the fire, and set them down carefully on top of the others. Gia glanced at him awkwardly about the seat and he waved it off then asked Marcy if he could squeeze in next to her. Marcy graciously obliged. Gia shot him a look and asked silently. *You okay?*

He nodded and smiled. He was fine.

The flames on the fire were growing smaller so he threw on another log. Everyone went back to chatting as Seth looked up and noticed the sky had gone black. He glanced over at Tom, now deeply involved in telling a funny story to the group on the other side of the fire, apparently.

"Excuse me a sec. I'll be right back," he said to Marcy. Seth made his way to the cooler. He took a deep breath and grabbed another beer.

"HEY, GIA," Tom whispered in her ear. "What do you even know about this guy?"

Gia raised an eyebrow. "You mean Seth?"

Tom nodded.

"What? He's totally nice. Just give him a chance."

They both looked over again and Gia watched as Seth sat back down next to Marcy and started up a conversation. Gia smiled. Marcy knew most people in town and Gia guessed they'd exchange stories and find something or someone in common.

At least he was getting along with her friends. Kira and Courtney had spread the word that Gia had invited a guy she liked tonight, so she knew Marcy would have her back.

Seth must have felt Gia's gaze, because he looked over and winked at her again. She tilted her head and smiled as Marcy continued talking enthusiastically about something, complete with hand gestures.

Tom saw the look they exchanged and put his arm around Gia. "Honey, you know I'm your friend, right? You know you can trust me?"

Was it Tom's two or three beers talking? Because he seemed a bit worked up. "Of course, Tom." She glanced back at Seth. Did he look a little uncomfortable at the closeness on display between her and Tom? She smiled to reassure him.

"Listen. Are you guys dating?" Tom asked, noticing the exchange between her and Seth.

"Uh, well, no." Gia turned her full attention to Tom. "But this probably isn't the best topic of conversation for *us*. I mean—after our talk last week."

And things were going so well between her and Seth tonight—it was only a matter of time now before he asked her out. She was sure of it. But Tom was the last person with whom she should be discussing this.

Tom sighed.

"Look, Seth and I are just friends. And don't worry—I can take care of myself." She'd been afraid he'd have something to say about Seth. Tom was not going to be a fan of Seth right now—no matter what was or wasn't going on between Seth and her. Until maybe Tom found himself a nice girl...

"All right, but listen." Tom sighed again. "Maybe you're right. Maybe I'm not the most objective I've ever been in my life. Just be careful. I don't trust him."

Gia pursed her lips and scolded him with a look. "Tom, you're being too protective. You've never even met him. Now go find a cute girl to talk to. I met a few of Jake's friends over there. She motioned to the other side of the yard. Jake said most of them are single."

Seth seemed like the polar opposite of so many of the guys she'd dated, now that she'd gotten to know him. He seemed perfectly trustworthy. Tom was just jealous, but she couldn't do anything about that.

Tom looked around, frowning. "Fine. But remember what I told you. Keep your guard up."

Gia gave him a push. "Go on. Relax. Have fun."

"Fine." Tom stood up and headed off.

ELEVEN

The fire was burning bright and Seth noticed the seat next to Gia was empty again. Gia seemed to be involved in a conversation with Nick, Courtney, Jake, and Angela. He touched Marcy on the arm gently when their conversation hit a lull. "Hey, do you mind if I go see what Gia's up to?"

Marcy glanced over at Gia and smiled. "Not at all. You'd better." She gave Seth a knowing look. "Great talking to you."

"Likewise. Keep me posted on that job search. It would be awesome if you could get into the local school district." Marcy had told him she'd just completed her master's degree in education and was looking for a full-time job. If nothing came along, she'd be subbing until she found something, and she'd been toying with the idea of staying on in Heritage Bay for the fall.

"Thanks. I will." She smiled graciously and turned to talk to the couple on her other side.

Seth headed back toward Gia.

"Hey, stranger. How goes it?" Gia patted the seat next to her and he sat down.

"Great."

They caught up for a few moments then both stared into the fire. Gia hunched her shoulders against the chill.

"Are you cold?"

"A little, yeah."

"Here, take my jacket." He was fine, especially in front of the fire. Good thing he'd brought it.

She took it gratefully and he wrapped it around her shoulders.

Seth looked up at the dark sky. A half moon was visible behind the trees and the fire burned brightly, lighting up the night.

He gazed over at Gia—would it be so bad if he were to blur the lines of their professional partnership and ask her out? Would it jeopardize their working relationship? There'd be a lot at risk if things didn't work out. Still, he found himself wanting to be closer to her, anyway. He inched toward her and pressed his arm against hers to warm her up. "Better now?"

She smiled, rubbing her arm against his, and pulled the jacket tighter. "Yeah. I'm good."

He finished off his beer and cleared his throat. "So what's going on over here? Looks like something's brewing."

She chuckled. "Oh, it's just a heated debate about the best places to take a mountain bike around Chicago. Nick's from there, and Jake's visited several times, so the controversy is real." She grinned ironically.

Seth laughed. "I'd like to hear this, myself." They both directed their attention to the group.

"You cannot be serious right now," Angela sputtered. "That trail is narrow and full of roots."

"Exactly," Nick said.

"Who likes to ride on roots?"

"Who doesn't?" Nick shot back, grinning.

Angela laughed and stood up. "Who needs a refill?"

The night went on and Gia asked Seth more about his family and he asked about hers. They talked about their favorite things to do outside of work. Seth told her he loved going fishing on the lake, and Gia said that she loved to cook.

"Oh my gosh, I have to cook something for you!"

Seth smiled. "That would be great."

"Tell me what you like and I'll make you something one night."

"Will you, really? Because my mom's a sweetheart and I love her cooking, but I'd love a change. I'm not proud of it, but I got a little bit spoiled in Sonoma. Dude, the food and the wine there—there's nothing like it."

Gia laughed. "With that five-star frame of reference, you're not going to like my cooking. I promise you."

Seth smiled big. "No, I promise *you*—I'm going to love your cooking."

"Okay then," Gia said, half teasing. "I'll figure out something soon then."

"Deal. Just tell me where and when and I will be there."

"Or be square." Gia threw back the last sip of her lager.

About half an hour passed and Gia said she was going to find the restroom in Jake's house. "I'll be right back."

"No worries." Seth hopped up and made his way to the cooler where he grabbed a bottle of water. He was having a great time. Gia was always so much fun to talk to.

He turned to head back to his seat at the fire when Tom approached him again. "Hey dude, can we talk for a second?"

"Yeah, sure." Seth glanced at Tom, whose feet were

planted wide and his shoulders rigid. "What's up?" Seth asked, not sure what to make of it.

"Look, I've seen the way you've been acting around Gia all night." He raised his head. "She obviously likes you."

What did he mean by that? And what was this guy's deal? Why was he telling him this? Seth shrugged. "Yeah. So? I like her, too. We work together, and we're friends."

"So—I don't want to see her get hurt. You've got a girlfriend, dude, and that's not cool—you're playing her. You're playing them both." Tom stepped forward. "Gia's going to be devastated when she finds out—I know her. And I don't like people messing with her."

Seth took half a step back. It wasn't worth causing a scene, plus, Tom was way off. "Look, I don't know what you think's going on here, but Gia and I are just friends. Anyway, this is none of your business. But I'm not *playing* anybody."

Tom didn't move. "Drop the act, dude."

Seth squared his shoulders and glared at Tom.

"She's into you, and she thinks you're—shall we say—available." Tom moved in closer so no one else would hear. "I suggest you tell her the truth ASAP before she gets her heart broken."

Seth let Tom's words sink in without replying. Gia was interested in him? Since when? And how did he not know this?

Seth held his gaze, breathing through his nose as Tom scowled and returned to the fire.

He was chugging his bottle of water when he saw Gia strolling toward him.

"Hey, whatcha doin'?" she said.

He put the lid on the empty bottle then tossed it in the recycle bin, his face clouded with concern. He wondered if

Gia had any idea about Stacey—would Tom have told her? He shook it off. "Oh, nothing. I just needed a water. You all set?"

"Yeah." She smiled—that beautiful smile again. Could it be true? Could she really be into him?

"Hey, you want to walk a little?" He needed to figure this out—now. Maybe he'd been misreading signals. Maybe he'd been sending signals he hadn't meant to, even before he broke up with Stacey.

"Sure." Gia fell in beside him.

Had she been hoping for something more from him all this time? If Tom had told her that Seth had a girlfriend and she'd thought he was interested in her at the same time, then he would've sounded like a player—and that just wasn't who he was. He couldn't let Gia maintain that impression of him, especially now that he knew she liked him—if that was even true. He had to let her know there'd been none of that, and he'd never cheat.

And he had to find out if she liked him. But how?

Seth swallowed over the lump that had formed in his throat as they walked a short distance from the crowd. Another couple had drifted off to the edge of the yard to steal a kiss in the dark. He and Gia noticed them and they both turned away.

Seth could still see Gia's face by the shimmering moonlight that filtered through the trees. He stopped and turned to her. "Hey."

"What is it?" She stopped and looked up at him. "So what's going on?"

What should he say? How should he say this? He could start by explaining his breakup with Stacey. She deserved to know about her, even though it was over. Especially after everything he'd shared with Gia about his time in Sonoma and his life since then. But in all fairness, he'd never even thought to bother her with the whole Stacey thing. He and Gia weren't really *there* yet as friends. Heading there, maybe, but not there yet. But if she really did have feelings for him like Tom had said, then...

"I have to tell you something." He studied her face in the moonlight. Tenderness, affection—it was there, wasn't it? He felt it. Could it be true?

He gazed down at her porcelain skin, her soft pink lips in the low light.

"What is it? What's wrong, Seth?" Gia's face was taut. "Did something happen?"

She was really—so beautiful. He honestly wanted to wrap his arms around her right then. "No. No, nothing like that. It's just—"

She was searching his face. He'd better just come right out with it all. His fingers itched to stroke her cheek. "There's something I haven't told you."

GIA GAZED into his deep-brown eyes. "Okay." Her heart pounded. It was finally happening, wasn't it? He was going to tell her he felt the same way about her that she felt about him. She reached out and softly took hold of his forearm. "What is it? You can tell me."

"Okay." He cast his gaze to the ground. "First of all, this has been on my mind constantly lately—I need to apologize to you first. I probably should've told you this before, but I've tried to keep my personal life separate from my professional life. It's just that we became friends pretty quickly..."

He *was* going to tell her he liked her. She could feel it.

She felt the strength of his forearm. She wanted to stroke it and pull herself closer to him. He smelled so good.

He went on. "But still, I just—I couldn't find a way to make it an appropriate conversation."

"What is it?" Gia said slowly, trying to be patient. She swallowed.

He looked back into her eyes. "Okay, here it is. I had a serious girlfriend—in California—and I just broke up with her. We'd been dating since I moved back here. I probably should've told you before. I didn't want you to get the wrong idea about us. I'm sorry."

Gia's eyes flew wide and she sucked in a breath. "You had a girlfriend?"

All this time? And apparently he knew she had feelings for him or he wouldn't have said she'd gotten the wrong idea. How on earth did she get this so wrong?

"Oh." She let out a breath, her heart beginning to pound. "Wow."

"I know, right? I didn't want you to think..."

Oh, gosh, he'd noticed her lingering glances, her tendency to hang around too long. He'd interpreted her interest in him correctly, but the feeling wasn't mutual. He'd been seeing someone else the whole time!

She had to say something. She couldn't let him know how this was affecting her. *Just play the friend.*

"So when did it happen—the breakup?"

"Sunday night."

Sunday night—the night after they'd sat outside his winery, talking and laughing all evening. She'd almost thought he might kiss her that night. What an idiot she was.

But why was he telling her all of this now?

Maybe because she'd practically been throwing herself at him for the past two weeks and it was his way of asking her to stop—without ruining their professional relationship? She was mortified. After all, they were doing great things together professionally. She'd become valuable to him because she could make him good money with the agency's well-paying event customers. She looked at the ground and took a small step backwards.

Courtney and Kira had been sure he liked her. What a fool she was! Her cheeks felt warm. This was definitely not what she'd expected to hear tonight.

And she wasn't about to ask who dumped whom. The girlfriend had probably broken it off, right? Or he wouldn't be upset enough to have told her about it tonight.

"Well, I'm so sorry to hear that. How long did you date her?"

"About a year."

Oh, my gosh. This was awkward beyond belief. She shook her head. *Just let him think you're the supportive shoulder to cry on.* That was the only way to save her dignity, right? "That's a really long time. I'm so sorry. Are you doing all right?"

"Oh, yeah. I'm fine. It was over between us, for a long time, really."

"Oh, okay, well that's good," she said clumsily. "I guess some things just aren't meant to be." Wasn't that the understatement of the year? She took off his jacket and handed it back to him.

He took it from her, hesitating. "I just didn't want you getting the wrong idea. We've had a really good working relationship going—and now, a friendship, I'd say. I just wanted to clear the air. I hope I didn't give you the wrong impression."

Oh, just shoot me now.

"Okay, so, uh, thanks for letting me know." Her cheeks

felt even warmer. She lowered her head. "Um, so I should probably get going."

She had to get out of there. Now.

He nodded but looked confused. "I'm sorry I didn't tell you sooner."

Gia shook her head. Her heart still pounded out of her chest. "It's okay, really. You're right—you're under no obligation to share your personal life with me. We're just business partners," she floundered. "I'd better go see if... Angela needs any help."

It was the only excuse she could think of. She hurried off. Pine needles crunched under her sandaled feet as she made her way back to the fire, where she slid in next to Kira.

Kira's brow tightened at her unusual approach. "Everything okay?"

"It's fine. I don't want to talk about it right now."

Kira put her arm around her and pushed some of her blanket over Gia's knees. "Okay, honey. No problem."

Gia still almost held her breath. What a fool she was.

A few minutes later, Seth walked back up to the crowd around the fire and found Jake. He stuck out a hand. "Hey, man. Thanks for having me. I'm gonna take off. Early morning tomorrow."

His voice sounded a little off, too. He was probably just as embarrassed as she was at the unpleasant conversation.

Why had he waited until tonight to tell her this? She never would've even invited him here if she'd known how uncomfortable she'd been making him.

Jake stood and shook his hand. "No worries. Glad you could make it. I'll see you around."

"All right, everybody, I'll see you later." Seth waved politely and made his exit, and they all said goodnight.

Gia's ears were still burning. Her cheeks were still probably bright red, too. Fortunately, probably no one could tell in the darkness.

Tom sat across the fire from her next to a girl that Jake had introduced earlier as a friend of his. Gia followed Tom's glance as he watched Seth leave. She met Tom's gaze then frowned and looked away.

She hated to think it, but Tom had been right. She should've listened.

TWELVE

Saturday morning arrived and Seth walked through the vineyard, checking the fruit's progress. The grass was still wet with dew, and the grapes were doing well. He flipped open the lid on his coffee mug and took a sip, then set it on the ground. He pulled a pair of pruning shears from his back pocket and clipped a young shoot from the vine. Summer pruning kept the vines healthier as they approached the fall harvest season. At least his vineyard was doing well.

But talk about botching things in his personal life. He'd tried to open up and be honest with Gia last night, and she'd run away, more or less. He'd thought she'd have been happy to hear he was no longer involved with someone. If she had, he would've told her how he'd been having feelings for her beyond that of a friendship, but she'd behaved so strangely, it hadn't felt like the right thing to do.

Honestly, what had even happened? He still wasn't sure. Did she not have a mutual interest in him? He'd thought for sure he'd read all the signs right—that she felt it between them, too. And her friend, Tom, however aggressively, had even told him as much.

She must've assumed exactly what he'd been trying to prevent her from thinking: that he was a cheater who'd been going behind his girlfriend's back to spend time with her. Tom had probably been feeding her that kind of message all night. He probably had also told her by now that they'd talked. So Gia had probably assumed Seth wouldn't have told Gia about Stacey if Tom hadn't pressured him into it.

But that wasn't it at all. What a mess.

Seth clipped off another small section of the vine.

He'd hightailed it out of there after he and Gia had talked, confused, embarrassed. What had all of those people thought of him when he'd emerged from the darkness alone after Gia had rushed out ahead of him? They'd probably thought the worst. And what had she told them after he'd left?

So much for making a few new friends around here. Oh well, he could handle the humiliation. He hadn't done anything wrong, after all—other than screw up his friendship and his chances with the woman he'd truly begun to care about.

He'd totally fumbled the ball with her.

He stared off into the orchard, thinking.

Things were going to be awkward between them now, weren't they? And just as soon as his chance with her had come along, it had gone. Just like that.

He glanced away from the orchard at the gray skies overhead. What was he supposed to do now?

This was going to affect their working relationship, but they both had too much on the line for that. They'd have to find a way to work things out, even if she had no feelings for him, after all.

He shook his head.

Stacey had called him late last night, too, after he'd gotten back from the bonfire. She wanted to rehash the whole breakup thing, but he'd been clear that nothing had changed.

He'd apologized again and consoled her. When was she going to accept it and start moving on? He wanted to leave their relationship in the past so he could move on, himself.

An image of Gia flashed across his mind, standing there in the moonlight last night. So lovely, so caring. *She* was supposed to be a part of his future.

Aw, heck. So what—about the working relationship. Not even twenty-four hours had passed since he'd talked to her and he missed her already. He didn't want to lose her. He shoved the pruning shears back inside his pocket and marched back to the warehouse.

GIA SAT ON HER COUCH, staring into space. She'd helped Jackie with another wedding today. Noreen had her on the schedule to help with weddings on most Saturdays this summer, and Gia knew it was for the best—she needed all the practice she could get. But once the cake had been cut, Jackie had sent her home. The rest of the evening would be easy. She hadn't needed Gia to stay.

Fortunately, the day had been busy enough that Gia hadn't been able to dwell on last night. She'd left shortly after Seth had, not wanting to talk about it even with the girls. But now, her thoughts swirled.

How had she misinterpreted things with Seth so badly? And how was she going to look at him from now on and pretend she hadn't been falling for him?

She drew in a heavy breath and looked up as her phone buzzed.

Tom's name flashed across the screen. She picked the phone up from the coffee table. "Hey, Tom," she said, trying to disguise the dismay in her voice. "How's it going?"

"It's going," he said matter-of-factly. "So what happened last night? Are you upset?"

She sighed. "I am. A little."

"I saw him leave."

She huffed softly. "I know."

"So let's hear it. What'd he say?"

Gia sighed. As much as she didn't want to tell Tom he'd been right, she could use a shoulder to cry on, even if it was only over the phone.

"Okay. So you know how I told you he was so honest and forthcoming and that I had nothing to worry about?"

"How could I forget?" Tom said.

Gia hesitated. "That was all, sadly, not the story. He had a girlfriend all this time, until just recently. He broke up with her last weekend."

Tom went quiet for a beat. "And?"

"And I've been flirting with him and making a fool of myself because I liked him, thinking he was single. He only told me so I wouldn't *get the wrong idea*—his words. Apparently, I've had the wrong idea all along. I wish I had known a lot sooner."

"Oh, honey, I'm so sorry. But I'm sure you didn't make a fool of yourself. It's not even possible. You're enchanting. Men fall under your spell. We're hopeless around you."

If only that were true. Gia smiled in spite of herself. Tom always cheered her up when she needed it.

"So they're broken up?" Tom asked.

"Yeah. I didn't get any details. He just said things

weren't working out for them." She sighed. "I feel like such an idiot."

Tom cleared his throat. "I'm so sorry, sweetie. Did he say anything else?"

"Not really. Just kind of made it clear I should back off."

Tom was quiet for a moment. "*So* not cool."

"Don't say *I told you so*."

"I won't."

Gia was glad to have Tom for a friend. She took a pillow from the couch and hugged it against her chest then pulled her bare feet up onto the seat.

"I feel so ridiculous. I should've asked him straight out if he was involved with anyone before I went and got my hopes up. I mean—he never made a move or anything. It just seemed like—well, we just seemed to click. That's all. I thought he wanted to start out as friends and see what developed. It sounds so stupid now when I say it out loud. I should've realized something was up."

She'd gone and done it again—like so many times before, allowing her generous and trusting nature to steer the wheel. She'd assumed that Seth was being completely upfront and forthright when he'd asked her to hang out with him or celebrate a great turnout at the festival. He might've even been planning to hit on her while he was still with his girlfriend, come to think of it! But the girl had apparently dumped him before he could.

And all this time, Gia had questioned nothing. When was she going to learn?

"It doesn't sound stupid." Tom's voice was compassionate. "He shouldn't have messed with your head. He was leading you on by not telling you."

Gia was quiet again. "I know. It kinda feels like that, too."

Gia switched the phone from one ear to the other. "Anyway, thanks, sweetie." She sniffled. "I guess I'm glad I know, now. It's better than carrying on like a fool."

Tom was quiet on the other end again before he spoke. "Are you gonna be all right? I can come over tonight and bring some ice cream. We can watch old movies and drink too much—get over this in record time?"

Gia laughed half-heartedly. "No, it's okay. But thanks. Kira and Marcy are coming over later. I'm sure they'll cheer me up. I'll take a rain check for the next time I do something stupid, though. Okay?"

He laughed. "You didn't do anything stupid, Gia. Guys are trouble. Don't ever forget that. Except me."

Gia chuckled and took a deep breath. "You really are one of the good ones, aren't you?"

"If only you'd give me a chance."

She laughed.

"Well, thanks. I'm glad you called."

"Anytime—seriously. You know where to find me. I'll talk to you later." He hung up.

SUNDAY FUNDAY IT WAS NOT. But nothing like a hearty meal to improve a lousy Sunday morning mood. Seth came in from the orchard and sat down at the breakfast table. His mother had scrambled some eggs for him. She was still frying up some bacon, and it smelled heavenly. His father had been served only egg whites and turkey sausages and had already headed out for a look at the vineyard.

"So how was the bonfire last night?" she asked pleasantly.

He shrugged. "It was good, for a while. Lots of nice people."

"That's good. But why only for a while?"

"Because the whole thing went downhill quickly after..." He frowned. "Ugh, you don't want to hear about it, Mom."

But he knew better than that. His mother loved to hear about the women he dated. She always brought up the fact that his father and she needed grandchildren in order to keep the farm in the family, and if he didn't get his act together, the family legacy might end with him since his younger brother and sister had turned their noses up at the agricultural lifestyle. He chuckled when she brought up exactly that line of debate, but still, she didn't need to hear about the mess he'd made of his friendship with Gia.

"After what? Try me." If there was one thing his mother was, it was persistent.

Oh, well, at least she was always there to listen. Maybe she could help him make sense of Gia's odd behavior.

"Okay, so this friend of Gia's thought I was playing with Gia's head. Thought I was trying to date her while I was still seeing Stacey. It's a long story—but he knew about Stacey because of the apartment she almost rented."

His mother looked concerned. "You're not getting back together with Stacey, are you?"

She'd only met Stacey once over a video chat, not long after he'd moved home to Wisconsin. She hadn't been very impressed with her, either.

"Nope—no chance of that. Don't worry."

She and his father had been quite pleased when Seth told them he'd broken it off with her. Her face relaxed. "Well, that's a relief."

Seth finished his eggs and toast then walked over and

leaned against the counter so he could hear his mother better over the crackling of the bacon grease.

"So *were* you trying to date Gia while you were still involved with Stacey?"

"Come on, Mom. Of course not. She's just a friend."

His mother eyed him.

"I mean, I'd like to date Gia now, but I wasn't up to anything like that. You raised me better than that."

She smiled. "Darned right I did. Well, you certainly could do worse. Gia's a genuine, hardworking Midwestern girl with good values, and she's right here, Seth—not off in another state that might as well be a lifetime away. Why don't you ask her out? I could see the sparks flying between you two last weekend."

"What are you talking about? You only met her for a few minutes. How could you have seen any sparks flying?"

"Believe me, young man, I know sparks when I see them. She likes you." Clara turned off the burner, took the bacon from the stove, and placed it on a paper-towel-lined plate to soak up the grease.

Seth took a piece and laughed. "Thanks. But I don't think she does."

"You're welcome." She turned to look her son in the eye. "My dear boy, are you blind? That girl stayed all evening out of the goodness of her heart for no other reason than to help you sell cherry pies. What attractive, young, single woman volunteers to spend her Saturday night doing that if she doesn't have some ulterior motive, however innocent it might be?"

Seth put more bacon on his plate and set it on the table again, then sat down.

"What are you saying? What kind of motive?"

"A crush—on you!" She threw her hands in the air then swatted his shoulder affectionately.

"You think so?" Apparently, Tom saw it and his mother saw it, but he—blind as a bat—still hadn't been sure he'd seen any signs that she was interested in him in that way.

"That's where you're wrong, Mom. I tried to tell her last night, and she took off."

"What do you mean—*took off*? What did you try to tell her, exactly?"

This was probably going further than he'd like when it came to mother-son conversations. "Never mind, Mom. It's over and done with now." He took a bite of the bacon—salty and delicious. Perfect.

His mother had definitely given him something to think about, though. Maybe he could talk to Gia, but what would he say?

She sighed heavily and stared at him. "What did you tell her?"

Seth sighed, too. "Okay, okay. I told her I'd just broken up with a serious girlfriend, and that I hadn't meant to give her the wrong idea about things."

His mother blinked. "You said what, now?"

Seth was defensive. "Well, I guess I've been interested in her, too, and if she could tell, then I didn't want her thinking I planned to try and cheat on Stacey with her. Women don't generally like to be *the other* woman."

His mother continued to stare at him. "Honestly, Seth, sometimes I think you're hopeless." She turned back to the stove and took the scrambled egg saucepan to the sink.

He swallowed and sat back. "What? Why?"

She continued to tidy up. "Did you tell her how you feel? Did you tell her anything about how you'd like to take her out on a date?"

"I never got the chance to. That's what I mean—she just kind of got weird and ran off to her friends, so I left."

She turned back to look at him. "That's because she probably has no idea that you even like her, if you never even said so!" His mother sighed again and sat down at the table. "Do I need to spell it out for you?"

He stared at her and grinned. "Apparently." Maybe he really *had* missed something there.

His mother smiled facetiously and attempted a patient tone. "Seth, what's a girl to think when a boy tells her he's been giving her the wrong idea? She's going to think he doesn't like her back, and then she's probably going to feel humiliated for displaying an interest in him. Honestly, son, didn't your father teach you anything besides how to run a tractor?"

Seth's mouth fell open. He knew his mother didn't actually mean that about the tractor. She had a flair for the dramatic.

But was she right? Had Gia totally misunderstood what he'd been trying to tell her last night? It would certainly explain why she'd run off the way she had, if he'd made her think the attraction wasn't mutual, with all the talk about Stacey.

He bit into another slice of bacon and recalled their conversation in the dark. The look on her face—her awkward questions. He took a long gulp of his second cup of coffee and set it back down.

Oh, for Pete's sake—his mother was right.

GIA'S HAIR blew out of place as she walked along a quiet beach early on Sunday afternoon, contemplating Seth's words at the bonfire. The air felt fresh and traces of wispy clouds filled the sky. She gazed out at the dark waters on the horizon, holding her sandals by the straps as the cool water washed across her ankles.

How did she always manage to get herself into these kinds of situations when it came to men? Ones in which she'd put her heart on the line and then had the rug pulled out from under her.

She bent at the knee and traced random lines in the sand with a twig. At least she knew where they stood now, and she wouldn't continue to make a fool of herself when she had to see him at the events she'd be running on his property.

Look on the bright side.

She wrinkled up her nose. It had become clear why people always said not to mix business with pleasure. Abundantly.

Still, would she ever be able to think of him as nothing more than a friend? She sighed and stopped to dig her toes into the sand.

If so, she wasn't sure how.

Kira and Marcy had talked her out of her lousy mood last night. They'd said she'd get over him, that she'd be able to handle being *just friends* with him—just give it time. But she wasn't sure how. She wasn't even sure *if*.

Her phone trilled from the canvas bag on her shoulder and she pulled it out to take a look. She stared at it. That couldn't be right.

But there it was. A text. From Seth.

Can we talk?

Gia gazed at the phone, her pulse quickening. Of course

she wanted to talk. She already missed him. But—should she even respond? It was just going to mean more humiliation and heartbreak for her. No good could come from her becoming more attached to him now.

But what if it was about a job? She couldn't just ignore him.

Does it pertain to one of our events?

Gia glanced out at the water, trying to keep a cool head. The lake was vast, full of mystery and danger. A lot like the status of her relationship with the hot guy she was crushing on. His answer came in quickly.

No, it's something else. I'm in town. Can I meet you somewhere?

She worried her lip. What else could he possibly want to talk about after the other night? She couldn't bear to hear anymore about this ex-girlfriend of his. To know his heart belonged to someone else...

But she'd have to find a way to be around him, if only for the sake of her job. She texted back before she could change her mind.

Okay. I'm at the north end of Harris Beach. I'll wait for you here.

TEN MINUTES LATER, Seth parked his truck on a side street and stepped out onto the sand in a pair of flip-flops. There she was, in a knee-length white skirt and tank top, her hair blowing in the wind. The picture of summer. The definition of beautiful. He swallowed hard, straightened his shoulders, and moved toward her. Would she be willing to listen to him? What an idiot he'd been. What she must think of him right now...

She stood up when he reached her. "Hi." A fake smile—he could tell. But just the fact that she'd agreed to see him was good enough.

"Thanks for meeting me. Do you want to walk?" he ventured.

"Yeah."

Seth fell in next to her, and they ambled across the sand. "So—I want to apologize again, Gia. I'm so sorry for not telling you about this sooner. I've been thinking of you as a friend since—almost since I met you—and friends tell each other these kinds of things."

Gia nodded. "It's okay. I'm not upset."

He didn't believe that for a second.

"You're not?" Seth glanced over at her.

She shook her head.

"Well, I still need to explain."

She stared at the shoreline as she walked. "Go ahead."

"I wanted to talk about it with you so many times, but this thing with Stacey—sorry, that's her name..."

Gia nodded again. "It's okay."

"It was serious for a long time between us. We were making plans to move forward, even though I had a lot of misgivings." He glanced off at the lake. "Before you even came along, though, things had already been going downhill between her and me—for weeks, months even. But she was so intent on making it work, I didn't know how to tell her I was nervous about it. I thought I should just give it a chance. I never had a girlfriend for that long. I figured cold feet were just a part of the game."

He stopped to read her reaction. She seemed a little surprised at what he was saying. "But then you came along two weeks ago, and I started seeing things through an entirely different lens."

Gia shook her head. "It's fine. Look, I understand about...Stacey. You don't need to get into it."

"Good." He stopped walking and stood in the wet sand where the water rolled up onto the beach and washed over their feet. "But do you understand how badly I handled things the other night?"

Gia stopped and looked up at him, her face searching his. "What do you mean?"

"I was trying to tell you something else the other night, but you left before I could. I think you got the wrong impression about what I was trying to tell you."

Her face fell. "No, I get that. We're just friends—you don't see me in any other way. I got it. Crystal clear." She frowned and looked away.

He wanted to take her hands in his—the urge was just as strong as it had been last weekend after the festival. He grabbed them. They felt warm and soft and she looked up at him, surprised. "No, not that wrong impression. The one where you think I only see you as a friend."

"What?" She looked confused.

He was bumbling this again. Slow down. *Keep it simple, stupid.*

"Gia, I'm totally attracted to you. That's what I was trying to tell you the other night..."

"You were?"

Seth nodded. "Yes."

She spoke almost in a whisper. "But you—but I didn't give you a chance?"

He nodded. "When I finally thought about what I told you, I realized that you must've misunderstood me. I was an idiot. I should've gotten right to the point. I'm so sorry I put you through all of that."

He squeezed her hands.

Gia kept her eyes on him, her expression lightening. She smiled. "Really? Because I thought…"

He held her gaze. "I know. You thought wrong." He smiled.

She stared at him, stunned.

He held her hands more tightly. "I like you, Gia. I want to get to know you better. Would that be okay?"

She still looked a little shocked, but she nodded eagerly. She leaned in more closely and he reached down and pressed his lips against hers.

She kissed him back. It was happening, and it was incredible. Her lips felt tender, gentle, understanding. Finally, he pulled away.

"Can you forgive me for making such a mess of things?"

"Of course I can." She reached up and kissed him again then wrapped her arms around him and he pulled her in.

THIRTEEN

Gia sat on the modern blue sectional in Mrs. Trewet's spacious living room. The anniversary party at the orchard was two weeks away and Abigail Trewet wanted to go over the seating arrangements.

There would be twenty tables with ten guests each, situated evenly around a rectangular dance floor. Next to that a small stage would be set up for a cover band that would play well-known hits from the last five decades.

Tim Trewet owned a fleet of popular sport-fishing boats in the area. Generations of Trewets had put down roots in the county, most of them in the commercial fishing industry in one way or the other.

Abigail was excited. "Tim is going to love it. Now, who is sitting where?" She peered at the floor plan on Gia's laptop.

"Well, Jackie said that your family members wanted to sit with friends and family they won't have seen in a while, and that you wanted to seat people according to their generation so they can catch up? You'll have plenty of time for mingling before and after dinner."

Abigail nodded.

"So we've got your closest friends and family members, according to the list you gave us, clustered here." She pointed to the six tables nearest Abigail's.

"Okay, perfect."

"And then your children and their spouses at these tables on both sides of the dance floor, with your grandchildren at this table."

"Right." Abigail was pleased. With Jackie's detailed plans, everything was falling into place.

"And then the other members of the community with whom Tim has had a solid business or personal relationship over the years, seated on this side."

"Okay, wonderful. That's exactly what I was hoping to hear. You're doing a fine job, Gia."

Gia smiled, relieved that Abigail hadn't changed her mind on any key points. Most clients had a major thing or two they wanted to change the closer it got to the date of an event. "And you've received just about all of your RSVPs, right?"

"Yes, all but maybe five or six."

"Okay, well that will do. I'll give the caterer the numbers by the end of the week. Let me know if you get any more, but I'm sure they'll plan for a few extra just to be safe."

"Yes, I certainly will. That sounds great."

"Well then, I'll be on my way." Gia closed the laptop and stood up. "I'll be in touch with any more details as they come up. It's going to be a wonderful party."

"Thank you! I'm sure it will and I'm looking forward to it." Abigail walked Gia to the door.

Gia said goodbye and settled into her car to head back to the office. Everything was finally falling into place.

Plans for the party were all set, and she and Seth were dating.

Two more days had flown by since the walk on the beach when he'd revealed his feelings for her. Two more blissful days.

They'd kicked back on the sand, talking for hours after Seth had confessed his feelings for her. The conversation had continued over dinner that night before a parting kiss, both of them ridiculously happy.

Yesterday, after work, he'd come to see her apartment. She and Seth had sat close and chatted on her couch all evening, completely wrapped up in each other. Gia sighed, remembering the way he'd kissed her goodnight. Seth was just so amazing. She couldn't get enough of him.

He'd brought cherry scones from the orchard's bakery for her to share with the team at the office this morning, which the women had loved. Buying points with the boss and her colleagues was always a good thing, although she hadn't told them she was dating him. Noreen had figured it was a thank-you for the October wedding she'd thrown his way.

He said he loved her place. It was cozy and tastefully arranged—his words. He hadn't stayed late because they both had to work in the morning.

Tonight, she'd met Courtney and Kira for a run, and he had to be up earlier than usual on Wednesday morning, so they weren't getting together.

Gia finished cleaning up the kitchen when her phone rang. She dropped the towel on the counter and picked up the phone.

"Hey there, beautiful." It was Seth.

"Hi." Gia blushed, even over the phone, when he said things like that. "How are you?"

"Great. Busy day. I've just been getting caught up on things around here." Seth explained what had been going on and Gia told him about her day, which had been, not surprisingly, very good. She was riding high on the wave of infatuation this week, and she knew it. It was a fun wave to ride.

"So I was just thinking about you..." he said.

"Were you?" She chewed on a fingernail.

"Actually, I've been thinking about you all day. But in this instance, I was thinking about when I get to see you next, and how I want to take you *everywhere* around here. I haven't had a chance to go anywhere since I've been back. Do you want to take a little road trip? I mean—just a day trip, around the peninsula?"

Did she, ever! "I would love to! There are so many places I've seen just in passing when I've worked weddings and other events, but I never get to stop and really check them out. Could we do that?"

"That's exactly what I was hoping you'd say."

"Okay, so what did you have in mind?"

"Well, a lot of things, actually, but—my first idea was to explore the wineries around here. I've been dying to see what's been going on locally since I've been gone for so many years."

"Keep talking." Gia smiled. "I love the sound of that."

"Have you been to any of the wineries on the Door County Wine Trail besides ours?"

"I haven't, and I would love to check them out!" Wine-tasting with her own private wine expert. How lucky was she?

"Great! Are you free on Saturday?"

"Yes, I actually am. I don't have any weddings that I

need to help with this Saturday, which is so rare right now. I've got one Friday and one Sunday, though."

"Okay, well that works out perfectly. I'll pick you up at eleven? We should have time to visit two of them, probably, and make another stop or two, plus dinner. I promise I won't have you back too late."

It sounded so romantic. Gia sat down at her kitchen table. "That sounds great. I'll see you at eleven."

"Cool. But hey, can I see you before then? I'm not sure I can wait four whole days."

He wasn't the only one. "I was just thinking the same thing."

He chuckled. "Good. How's Thursday after work? Maybe we can just take a walk or something?"

Oh, if he didn't know how to treat a lady! "I would love that. But I'll make us a quick dinner first. Nothing fancy. Come over around six thirty."

"All right, now you're spoiling me."

Gia couldn't stop grinning. "Someone's got to."

"How did I get so lucky?" Seth's tone was sweet.

"I could ask you the same thing." Her heart raced. She thought she might burst at the seams.

"Okay, thanks. I would love that. I'll see you Thursday, then."

SETH STOOD in Gia's doorway in a pair of Bermuda shorts and a cream-colored linen shirt on Thursday evening, holding a bouquet of colorful flowers.

"They're beautiful! That was so sweet of you. Thank you!" What a romantic gesture. How lucky was she?

He kissed her softly and she took the flowers from him, beaming.

"It smells so good in here. What did you make?"

"Just my balsamic honey-glazed chicken. Do you like chicken?"

"Do I like chicken? Of course I like chicken."

She laughed and he kissed her again.

She found a vase in the kitchen and set the flowers down on the table.

Gia had sautéed the chicken portions and then drizzled them with her homemade glaze. She'd serve it over a bed of rice with a side of steamed vegetables. It really was an easy dish to whip up even at the last minute.

"I don't care what it is—I can't wait." He smiled. "But seriously, you didn't work too hard, did you?" He put his arms around her waist and she felt his breath on her neck.

"Not at all. Don't worry."

"Good. You already work hard enough as it is." He pulled her in close and kissed her slowly and for a few moments, she all but forgot about the food.

After dinner, Seth stood up to clear the plates from the table. "Let me take that for you. The chef shouldn't have to clear the table."

He was so sweet.

"That's okay. I'll get it." Gia reached for her plate. She hadn't intended for him to lift a finger tonight. Making dinner for him had been a delight.

"Nope. I insist." He took it from her and gently deposited both plates in the sink then came back for the rest of it, planting a kiss on her cheek before he walked away. "That was one of the best meals I've ever had. You weren't kidding when you said you could cook."

"I appreciate that, but it was easy."

He laughed. "I'm being serious. And if that was easy, I can't wait to taste *difficult*." He winked at her and she laughed then finished off the last few drops of the ice water in her glass. She got up from the table and walked over to the sink. She couldn't let him do all of this work on his own.

"No way, kid. You're not doing the dishes," Seth blocked her from the sink.

"But you're my guest."

"Don't care. But how about this: I'll wash, you dry, and then let's take that walk?"

Gia grinned. "Are you sure? I can leave them for later." Of course, she'd love it if she didn't have to come back to a sink full of dishes tonight.

"It'll take half the time if we do them together." He stood behind her and took her gently by the waist, then scooted her over, turned on the water, and soaped up the sponge.

Gia sighed with contentment, watching him start with the sauté pan. Was there anything sexier than a guy who didn't mind housework? She'd better look out because she was in big trouble.

GIA AND SETH strolled hand in hand behind the other patrons touring the Whistling Creek Winery on Saturday. The property was situated in the central interior of the peninsula, not too far from Heritage Bay. Seth was impressed with it.

A blanket of perfect green grass showcased a wide, modern structure with an A-frame roof and a rustic brown barn. A lazy creek flowed quietly past a lush vineyard and rows of leafy deciduous trees surrounded the estate in every direction. He was thrilled that Gia seemed to be enjoying herself so much. He was enjoying himself, too.

They'd sampled several of the wines in the tasting room first. Then they'd followed a guide through the vineyard and learned about the grape varieties that Whistling Creek specialized in. Next was a visit to the production room where the guide had shown them the ins and outs of the company's winemaking operations, and now, the tour was finishing up. It was time to sit back and enjoy the scenery, and the beautiful, sophisticated woman he'd come here with. They sat down.

Seth squeezed her hand. "This place has grown a lot in the past decade. I only visited once before, but that was at least five years ago."

"I find it fascinating—and delicious." Gia said. "I've never officially toured a winery before, other than yours, and I really had no idea how wine is made. Thanks for bringing me here."

He smiled and reached across the outdoor table and gave her a long, soft kiss on the lips. She tasted sweet, like the wine. "I'm glad you like it. I'd love to teach you more about it, myself."

"Let's do it. I want to learn."

"You've got it. Some weekend when you're not busy..."

"Sounds good."

Today, it felt like he'd been able to share a little bit of the life he'd had for the past nine years with her. He wished he could show her what it had been like in Sonoma. She'd love it there. But for now, this was the next best thing.

Seth had tried just a couple tastes of the wine since he was driving them around today. He chugged his glass of water. "Something about being out in this setting really makes me happy. Must be the familiarity of a place like this after all the time I spent in California wine country."

Gia nodded. "That makes sense, but I'm sure glad you're here in Wisconsin wine country now."

He pulled her closer. "So am I. I wouldn't want to be anywhere else."

Gosh, but that smile of hers was contagious.

Gia had another taster-sized sip of her red wine left. She drank it and sat forward then took his hands in hers. "Seth, I have to tell you, this week has been...well, I never thought..."

He sat forward, stroking the back of her hand softly as she went on. "I just didn't think you'd ever feel this way about me after we had that misunderstanding. And as surprised as I was about it that night at the bonfire, I'm really glad you told me about your ex-girlfriend. I'm also really glad that you handled things the way you did with her, because it shows me how honest and trustworthy you are. Those are the things I value the most when I'm seeing someone."

He liked that she could be so forward and honest about her needs. It showed a sense of maturity that he hadn't seen in a woman he was dating—well, in a long time. Again, how lucky was he?

Seth gave her hands a gentle squeeze. "So do I. I want you to trust me, Gia."

He was glad he'd kept his emotional distance from Gia until he'd broken up with Stacey. He had no regrets. And he had a clean conscience. That felt good.

"I do trust you." Gia reached out and ran her hand along his cheek. He raised his head and she looked him in the eye. "I wouldn't normally talk about something like this with someone I've only been dating for a week..." She stopped and smiled. "But since we were friends first, I feel like I know you better than, well, just a week's worth."

He nodded. "I know what you mean." He did know. Even though everything felt so new and exciting between them, they also felt comfortable and familiar, like they were old friends.

"Anyway, I just want to say that, in the past, I've been burned by guys I've trusted, too many times, and I don't ever want to get into that kind of a situation again."

Seth nodded.

"So if anything ever comes up, I just want you to feel like you can tell me about it. Tell me everything—I can handle it. Okay?"

He gazed back at her again. "I will. And I want you to do the same for me."

"I will." She smiled.

"Look, Gia, I'm all in. I really want this." He wrapped his hands around both of hers. "I really want *you*." He meant it. He was falling hard for this woman.

"Me, too," she said, and he knew she meant it.

A FEW HOURS later they'd stopped for a quick bite and a walk through a few shops in a tiny coastal village north of Anderson Cove. Gia took a few pictures of them before they continued on to the second winery. One, in front of the lake, and another, standing next to a fifty-year-old ship's anchor that had been set in stone as a memorial on the town's square. The day felt fresh and magical, full of exploration and new experiences.

This second winery's estate sat inland on the northwestern side of the peninsula and boasted lush grounds full of leafy trees and shade plants. Flowers provided bursts of color and a soft breeze blew, easing the humidity of the late afternoon.

Seth and Gia had sampled a few wines in the tasting room, talking and laughing, and now they strolled the property, checking out the view. His arm felt comfortable wrapped around her shoulders.

The main building was a modern take on an Italianesque design and featured a cozy restaurant with stone-fired pizza where they'd have a casual-but-romantic dinner later.

The birds chirped and the breeze blew softly. Gia stopped in front of a fountain. "Let's take another photo here."

Seth pulled her close and smiled as she aimed the phone at them. "That's a great shot. Will you send it to me later?"

She nodded.

They strolled further, away from the other guests to a more private spot in front of a small pond. Gia stopped to take a look around. "This is really nice. You ought to create some sort of walking path through the orchard for your winery guests."

"That's a great idea." Seth scratched the back of his head. "Right now, I mean—strolling the orchard is an option, but without any designated or obvious direction, I don't think many guests bother to try it." He nodded, thinking. "But it'd be easy enough to set up an actual path."

"And the orchard's every bit as lovely as these grounds, just with a whole different feel—the all-American farm."

"Thanks." He nodded. "That's what my dad was going for with the red barn when he remodeled it—the all-American farm." Seth smiled and looked at her. "Beautiful, smart, and full of great ideas. How did I get so lucky?"

She laughed. "Handsome, charming, talented. How did *I* get so lucky?"

He chuckled. "Touché." Seth stopped and wrapped his arms around her neck. "Honestly, Gia, I can't get enough of you." He brushed the blonde hair from her cheek and teased her lips with his.

She kissed him back softly. This might just be the most perfect day she'd ever imagined.

The evening sky closed in as they sat across the table from each other, sharing a pizza by candlelight and making plans for the things they wanted to see and do before the summer was out. Gia was over the moon, not sure if she'd ever come down.

FOURTEEN

On Sunday evening, Seth and his parents sat around the farmhouse table, eating dinner.

"So what's going on with you and Gia?" His mother wanted updates now that Seth was dating her. "Did you have a nice time yesterday?"

He certainly didn't mind talking about her. She was all he thought about, lately. "Yeah, we really did. She's a great girl."

His mother dished a serving of potatoes onto each of their plates. "Well, I'm glad you're finally taking a break and enjoying yourself a bit."

His father passed the salad to his mother, who took a serving then handed it along to Seth. "Your dad and I had been talking about it, and to be honest with you, honey, we're so glad you finally made the decision to end it with Stacey. We thought it was nonsense that she'd been planning to come like that in the first place. To move here without even visiting first just felt irresponsible. But we didn't want to stick our noses in."

"That's so unlike you, Mom." Seth grinned and his mother laughed.

"Your mother's right," his father said. "We won't need another employee in the fall when everything begins to slow down with the tourists. We weren't sure how we would even have paid her."

"I know, and you don't have to worry about that anymore." Seth took a bite of his salad. "I should've taken care of it long ago." He arched an eyebrow and took a bite of his pork chop. He hadn't realized his plans had been stressing them out so much. Well, that was all behind him now.

His mother wiped her mouth and nodded. "We're so happy you've found a nice girl, honey. It'll make your life so much easier in the long run that she's from around here."

"Well, she's from Minnesota, technically."

"That's still from around here, in my mind." His mother grinned and Seth nodded agreeably.

"When do I get to meet this girl?" his father asked.

"I'll bring her around soon."

His mother put down the bottle of dressing. "So how do you think our winery's looking after visiting a few others around here yesterday?"

Seth wiped his mouth. "Actually, it feels really modest in comparison, but the others gave me some ideas. Our wine's just as good as everything I sampled, though."

"And that's what counts." His father glanced over at Seth.

This morning, he'd told his father how the owner of the winery they'd visited yesterday had sent his regards. Seth mentioned the improvements that must've gone on in the time since he'd left and how he had some ideas to improve things here at the Pederson Winery to keep up with the competition.

"Absolutely." Seth took a sip of his water.

His parents both loved the idea of creating a dedicated walking trail for guests. It would encourage people to stay longer. Maybe they'd spend a little more money in the market, too.

He wanted to put benches in the orchard along the way. His mother suggested that the path should venture a short distance through the orchard, meander through the vineyard, and then wind around the market before it looped back to the barn. They could create a few focal points along the way with a birdbath and another flowering arbor, maybe some signage for taking selfies. Seth thought it was a great plan.

"So the anniversary party's coming up on Saturday. Dad, do you think you'll be feeling well enough to attend? We're all on the guest list."

"He'd better, because I don't want to be sitting alone." His mother chuckled.

"I'll be fine," his father sputtered. "I'm looking forward to seeing some old friends."

"Good." Seth placed another dollop of mashed potatoes on his plate.

He was looking forward to Saturday for many reasons, one of which was to see his parents relax and have a good time together. After all they'd been through lately, they deserved it.

He also was eager to see their first big event go off without a hitch. Noreen had called to schedule a corporate banquet and an angler club's annual picnic for the outdoor venue in August, and that was just the beginning.

But he couldn't deny it. He was most looking forward to

the party because he'd get to experience all of it working side by side with Gia Stewart. Doing the work he loved alongside the woman he cared for, maybe would even grow to—dare he think it?—love someday. It was too soon for that word, but his feelings were heading in that direction faster than he'd ever anticipated.

His misgivings about his future—they'd all disintegrated when he'd left Stacey and finally followed his instincts. No more feeling caught between two different worlds, no more constantly missing his old life in California, no more feeling like an outsider looking in anymore—which had been the strangest sensation, since he'd been born and raised here. Regardless, it was a relief to feel like he belonged here again.

The weight of the farm's financial problems were even lifting from his shoulders a bit, with high hopes for the future.

He was settling into his life here on the farm and he was finally content. He had Gia to thank for a lot of those things. She believed in him and she saw in him the person he wanted to be. He wanted to live up to those expectations.

MUSIC HUMMED over the sound system as Gia spoke into the waiter's ear. "A cosmopolitan, please." She had a two-drink limit, especially on weeknights, and tonight was a Tuesday.

Fortunately, tomorrow would be an easy day. The plans were set for the party at the orchard on Saturday and everything was moving along according to schedule. Just a few last-minute to-do lists to complete and she'd be ready. She was excited about it.

She stood chatting with Kira at The Anchor Bar & Grill, a popular spot in Heritage Bay where she regularly got together for drinks with friends. The Anchor had an air of sophistication without the pretentiousness found in some of the more urban establishments, but the vibe was youthful even with its cozy maritime memorabilia. Tonight the group had met up for happy hour. It was great to catch up with everyone.

Tom, Nick, and Jake sipped from their bottles of beer, commenting on the game that played on the flat screen TV over the bar, while Courtney, Marcy, and Angela sat around a table on the barstools they'd managed to snag. Gia had invited Seth to come, but he said he'd been exhausted and was going to call it an early night. He'd love to join them another time.

Gia had filled Kira in on the recent developments with Seth. "Oh, girl, that is so exciting!" She squeezed Gia's arm. "And see, Courtney and I called it. Hate to say I told you so, but I *knew* he liked you."

Gia switched her weight from one foot to the other and straightened her camisole strap. "That's the best kind of *I told you so*, though. I'm glad you were right."

"Is he a good kisser?"

"Kira—that is none of your business." Gia blushed, grinning.

"Okay. Well, I guess I'll just live vicariously through someone else, then, if you're not talking."

"Aw, don't you think it's about time you started meeting some new people, honey? I mean, Sam's been gone for almost two-and-a-half months. You're only young once. What harm would it do to start dating again?"

"I know," Kira said. "You're right, and that's why I gave my number to a guy I met last week on a job. He asked me out." She squeezed Gia's wrist. "He's super cute."

"You did? That's great! Has he called yet? Or texted?"

"Actually, yes, he has. He's taking me to dinner on Friday."

"No way? You were holding out on us! I'm telling Courtney." Gia turned to face Courtney.

"Courtney already knows. She was there!"

"And neither of you told me? I am so mad right now—at both of you!" Gia stared at Kira, grinning.

They walked over toward the table of girls and Kira laughed. "I'm sorry. I didn't want to get too excited until I went out with him. He might be a total snoozefest."

"Oh, that's true. It's best to wait and see before you get your hopes up. I certainly didn't exhibit that kind of willpower." She rolled her eyes. She'd been caught up in Seth right from the start.

Kira laughed. "Yeah, but it all worked out in the end. No harm, no foul."

"I'm like—so happy lately—I have to pinch myself sometimes."

Kira reached out and pinched her as they reached the table.

"Ouch!" She laughed. "What's this new guy's name, by the way?"

"Darren."

Gia turned to Courtney and the other girls. "So you all knew about Darren?"

Courtney, Angela, and Marcy all nodded.

"Yeah, we knew." Angela grinned. It's about time Kira got back in the game."

"And when were any of you going to tell me?"

Just then the guys strolled over to the table. Jake went

behind Angela and put his arms around her shoulders, laying a kiss on her cheek. Nick stood beside Courtney and she reached out and wrapped her hand around his generous bicep.

"What's goin' on, ladies?" Tom casually put an arm around Kira.

"Gia was just giving us a hard time for not telling her about the hottie I met last week." Kira took a sip of her drink.

"That's so unlike Gia." Tom glanced over at her with a grin. "And why was she giving you such a hard time? You deserve to find true happiness, Nash. Don't listen to Gia. She's such a downer."

Gia let out a huff, jokingly, and scrunched up her nose at Tom. "No one told me about it. Turns out I'm the last to know."

"That's only because you've been off in la-la land with Seth all week," Courtney chimed in. "Head in the clouds, ignoring the rest of us."

Gia protested. "I haven't been ignoring you guys, have I?"

Courtney laughed. "I'm just kidding. No, you have not, and you deserve it, Gia. We're all really happy for you."

Gia thanked her.

Tom rubbed his chin. "What are you talking about? What's going on with Seth?" He rested his gaze on Gia, his tone uncertain. "I thought you two were on the outs."

Angela jumped back in. "They were. But he set things straight and now they're dating. Isn't that fabulous?"

Tom looked distraught and removed his arm from Kira's shoulder.

Kira made a face to keep the mood light. "Letting you

two talk." She stepped out of the way and changed the subject at the table, and the laughter resumed.

Tom stepped toward Gia. "Can I talk to you for a minute?"

"Of course." She kept her voice down. "What's wrong?"

Gia knew exactly what was wrong. She hadn't yet told him about Seth because she wasn't sure how. It was either going to hurt him, or he was going to warn her away from Seth again, and she didn't want to deal with either of those things—at least not yet.

"What's this about you and Seth? Are you dating now?" He seemed agitated.

"Yeah, we are."

Tom nodded, his jaw clenching. "But—"

"I'm sorry, Tom. I appreciate how you helped me feel better last week, but what Angela said is true. He wasn't trying to go behind his girlfriend's back with me, and he wasn't trying to let me down easy that night. He was actually trying to tell me he likes me. It was all a big misunderstanding. We're together now."

Tom let it sink in. "Wow. Together." He nodded. "So, then—"

"I really like him, Tom. He's not what you think."

"And when were you planning on telling me? I thought we were friends. After all the times we talked about him..."

Gia frowned. He was right. "I owe you an apology, Tom. I should've called you." She grabbed his hand.

Tom shook his head and tried to brush it off but his tone was blunt. "It's fine. I hope it works out for you." He turned and walked away.

FIFTEEN

Gold was the traditional color for fifty years of marriage, and by four thirty on Saturday afternoon, elegant golden accents gleamed from sparkling white tablecloths atop every round table of ten at the Pederson Orchard's event space.

Gia checked her clipboard. Everything was under control. The caterers were running on schedule, the cake had arrived in one piece, and the band was finishing up its sound check. The table settings looked exquisite with their gold-rimmed white china. And tall bouquets of yellow roses and violets, the traditional fiftieth wedding anniversary flowers, filled a vase on every table.

Strings of outdoor white lights had been strung on gold-colored wires that led from the store building to the tents and on to the trees. It was going to look absolutely magical when the sun went down in a few hours. Gia was thrilled.

She dusted off her jeans and headed for the ladies' room to straighten her hair, change, and freshen up. She'd been there for three hours setting up and had worked up a sweat in the afternoon sun. Fortunately, the heat of the day was wearing off. Still, she needed to clean up and change into her cream-colored skirt and dressy pink top, along with a pair of pumps, before the guests arrived.

She changed her outfit, ran a brush through her hair, reapplied her makeup, and headed outside again. The guests would start arriving in about fifteen minutes.

Back at the banquet lawn, her eyes fell on Seth coming toward her from the farmhouse, impeccably dressed in a slim-fitting black suit that both enhanced his muscular build and showcased his refined taste. She drew in a breath. The dark tie he wore over a white button-down set off his clean-shaven, handsome face. She wanted to kiss him. Now.

But that would have to wait. His parents, also dressed smartly for the occasion, strolled along beside him.

Gia smiled and smoothed her skirt, trying to ignore the jitters that had just hijacked her system.

"Mrs. Pederson, so nice to see you again." Gia held out her hand and they shook.

"It's wonderful to see you, too, Gia. And please, call me Clara." She turned. "I don't think you've actually met my husband?"

Mr. Pederson reached out to shake her hand and answered for her. "No, but I've heard a lot about you." He winked at Seth. "Only good things. I'm John." He directed his gaze at the lawn. "And the setup here looks top-notch. Thanks for all of your hard work."

"My pleasure." Gia shook his hand warmly. "It's great to finally meet you. I've heard a lot of wonderful things about you, as well. Thank you for hosting the party tonight."

John smiled, and he and Clara said they'd see her later then moved on to wander among the tables for a look around.

Seth gave her a hug. "You look amazing."

Gia tilted her head to the side. "Thanks. But look who's talking." She eyed his outfit. "You clean up well."

"Thanks." He tugged on his sleeve, straightening the cufflink, and grinned. "I haven't been in a suit in months. Feels good."

"Glad to hear it." She cocked an eyebrow.

He kissed her lightly on the lips and her skin felt warm. But there would be time for more of that later. She straightened her shoulders and tossed back her hair.

"So is everything all set?" he asked.

She cleared her throat. "So far, so good. Everyone's been on time and the setup's gone well. We're almost ready."

"Well, it looks fantastic. You're incredible."

Gia beamed, hunching up her shoulders.

"Come here," he said, pulling her close. "I can't get enough of you right now." He held her tightly, and she breathed him in, closing her eyes and taking the moment to celebrate. The man of her dreams was holding her in a tender embrace. Was this even real?

She finally pulled back. "It wasn't all me, of course."

"It wasn't all you, Gia, but still, you made it all happen." He looked more serious for a moment. "And I hope you know how happy you make me—and not just because you can throw a good party." His grin was back.

Seth was right. She'd done a lot of the work, and she'd done a great job. Tonight's party was coming together as something to be proud of. But it wouldn't have meant half as much to her if he weren't a big part of her life.

She smiled. "I do." She kissed him softly again and then pulled back.

Seth stretched his shoulders. "Okay, I have to go check on a few things over in the warehouse and then make a couple of quick phone calls to a supplier before the party starts. I'll be back in a little bit. I wanted to get my mom and dad over here early and make sure you were doing all right."

"Okay. Thanks. I'll see you soon." Gia checked her watch. She always wore a watch on event nights.

He started to walk away. "Oh, and hey…"

Gia turned. "Yes?"

"Will you dance with me tonight when they play a slow song?"

Gia's face relaxed into a smile.

An event planner didn't normally dance at the parties she was throwing, but an exception could be made, right? Most women in the field weren't dating the owner of the venue where their event was being held. This was Seth's family's home, and after all, he was on the guest list. Besides, Mrs. Trewet wouldn't mind. The woman was a hopeless romantic.

"I would love to."

"It's a date, then." Seth bit his lower lip, smiled at her, and hurried off.

Gia grinned and pulled out her clipboard again. She couldn't wait.

About ten minutes later, the first guests arrived and Gia greeted them, pointing them to the counter with the seating assignments.

An hour and a half later, everything was going according to plan. Mr. and Mrs. Trewet were animated, caught up in lively conversation with friends. Soft background music played. Guests mingled, chatting, sipping drinks, and sampling appetizers from trays being passed around by waitstaff. The Pederson's cherry wine was even available for guests, a last-minute change Abigail had wholeheartedly agreed to. Gia watched from the ground-level porch outside the farm store and breathed her first sigh of relief of the evening. Milepost number one—check.

Gia also noticed that Seth made an impressive host. He'd been chatting with dozens of people, making his way around the lawn to greet guests and introduce himself. He seemed to be doing his best to make the night a success and interest others who might want to throw a party at the orchard. Gia smiled, watching him shake hands and laugh.

Gia caught a whiff of the chicken entrée the caterers were cooking up in tents in the side parking lot. Dinner would be served soon so she'd better start directing the guests to the tables. Already, the first of the breadbaskets and salads were being brought out, and several people had noticed and begun to wander to their seats. But most had not. Convincing people to leave the open-bar area for the seated portion of the evening was often the most challenging part of an event.

She started toward the crowd when her phone trilled and stopped to grab it from her pocket as Tom's name lit up the screen. What did he want? To hash out her relationship with Seth again? It seemed like the only thing he wanted to discuss with her lately. She didn't have time for that conversation right now—however good his intentions might be. He'd have to wait. She could call him back tonight after the party, or tomorrow, since she'd probably get home late. This just wasn't the time.

Fifteen minutes later, the guests were enjoying their salads over lively table conversation. Seth had noticed Gia's attempts to corral them all and had lent a hand. He really had a wonderful comfort level with people, even in a crowd. She'd given him a silent *thank you* from afar and he'd returned a warm smile. He'd taken his seat at his parents' table on the far side of the lawn with several other longtime members of the agricultural community, where she guessed he'd be involved in a spirited discussion about something or other by now. He was a natural at hosting.

Gia returned to the porch where she could get out of the way while the caterers handled the meal. A few minutes later, she turned, surprised, as a young woman with long brown hair touched her on the arm. The woman was carrying an overnight bag and a handbag. It seemed strange she'd bring luggage here, but maybe she'd taken a cab and would be staying with friends for the night or something? She must not be from the area.

"Excuse me, but I just got into town. Can you point me to the family hosting the event?" She glanced across the wide lawn at the banquet in progress, clutching her bags.

"Sure," Gia said amiably, "and, welcome! But everyone's having dinner right now, so if you like, I can help you find your table and take you to the guests of honor later. Are you a family member or a friend of the Trewets?" She took a few steps toward the list of table assignments and the woman followed. So that explained the overnight bag.

"Oh, no, I'm sorry. I didn't mean the guests of honor. I meant the Pedersons."

Gia raised an eyebrow. The woman was about Gia's age. Tall, attractive, fashionably dressed. She hesitated. "Oh. All right." That was odd. Gia hadn't noticed an empty seat at the Pederson's table. "I'll check where you're supposed to be." She scanned the table assignments. "What's your name?"

"Uh, thanks. It's Stacey Lochner, but I'm not here for the party. I'm looking for Seth Pederson. Do you happen to know him?"

Gia's eyes went wide. "Uh, yes—I do," she stuttered, her pulse quickening. "Is he expecting you?"

Stacey. This was *Stacey*?

"Actually, no, he's not. I just flew in from California. It's a surprise. I'm kind of nervous to see him."

Oh my goodness. Seth said it was over between him and Stacey. What in the world was she doing here?

Gia glanced around. *Of all the...* This wasn't something she could allow to ruin tonight's event. Her heart began to pound.

"Look, uh, Seth is out there attending to guests. It's almost a *working* evening for him. I'm not sure he'd appreciate—"

"Oh, I get it. No problem. I didn't realize it would be tonight, although he told me about it a few weeks ago—is this the big anniversary party he's been planning? He was so excited about it the last time we talked about it."

"Yes, it is." Gia tried to keep a cool head. She chewed on her lip. What was Seth going to say to this?

"I can do a lap and find him if you don't know where he is." Stacey made a move toward the lawn.

"Oh no, don't do that," Gia answered quickly, stepping in front of her. "Please." She'd better do something before Stacey took it upon herself to hunt him down. Abigail and Tim Trewet would not appreciate the scene it might create. Now would Gia. "I'll go and get him for you. Please just make yourself comfortable here."

"Thank you." Stacey nodded and backed up against the wall.

Gia shuffled across the lawn, smiling at guests, noticing the music level was perfect for conversation and that everyone seemed to be having a great time. Servers cleared salad plates, refilled bread, and a few were already bringing out the main course. But the tips of Gia's ears burned and her cheeks felt hot.

She nodded at guests, plastering a smile across her face.

When she reached Seth's table, she approached casually. "Excuse me, Mr. Pederson, may I have a word with you? There's a small matter over in the..." She looked at the store's porch, swallowed, and allowed her voice to trail off.

Seth looked up. "Sure," he said with an air of concern. He wouldn't have seen Stacey yet—she was too far away. He stood and made a quick apology to the guests sitting next to him, and left his jacket to rest over the back of his chair. Clara and John glanced over, curious. Gia smiled at them and shook her head so as to reassure them.

"What is it?" Seth whispered.

Gia led the way across the lawn. "You're not going to believe this." Gia found she was having a hard time keeping her voice steady. But more than anything else at this point, she was concerned about the party. "Just promise me you won't let her make a scene."

Seth looked at Gia in confusion. "Who?"

Gia stared straight ahead. "Stacey."

Seth's eyes shot wide. "What?"

Gia swallowed again, nodding.

A moment later they reached the porch and Gia stopped. She nodded in Stacey's direction.

Seth stopped short and let his gaze cross the porch. The blood drained from his face.

SIXTEEN

Seth did a quick shake of his head and blinked a few times. "Stacey?" This couldn't be happening, could it?

Stacey hurried over. "There you are! Oh, Seth! I've missed you so much!" She threw her arms around his neck.

Seth's eyes went wide. He hugged her back stiffly, in shock.

Gia was right. This was no place to make a scene. But the porch was far enough removed from the banquet lawn that they'd mostly go unnoticed unless something highly unusual went on.

He pulled back and stared at Stacey. "What are you doing here?"

"What do you mean? I'm here to *see* you! I just flew into Milwaukee this morning."

Seth turned around to glance at Gia. She was standing just a few steps behind him, still clutching her clipboard, her eyes still as wide as his.

He turned back to look at Stacey. He couldn't let Gia get the wrong idea. He'd had absolutely no idea that Stacey was going to do this. Gia had better hear him say it right away, just for the record.

"But you didn't tell me—anything." Their conversation wouldn't be heard over the hum of the party and the music as long as he kept it cool. "What's this about? What are you doing here?"

Stacey tilted her head to one side and reached up to play with his tie. "That's no way to greet a girl who just flew two thousand miles to see you. I missed you, babe—and I wanted to show you what it would be like if I were here. You said you couldn't imagine me in Wisconsin, on your farm. So now—I'm here." She held out her arms to demonstrate. "You don't have to imagine anymore."

Seth's jaw dropped. "You've got to be kidding me." He cleared his throat and feigned another smile.

"I'm one hundred percent serious." Stacey threw her arms around his neck again and pulled herself toward him, planting a kiss on his lips before he knew what was happening.

He pulled away just in time to see Gia turn and flee. *Uh-oh.* He glanced around, trying to think straight.

What should he do? Stacey should know better than this. She'd worked enough weddings and parties at the Henderson Estates to know you didn't go putting your personal life front and center while you were working. She had to realize he was working tonight, even though he was also a party guest.

He cast his gaze off into the distance and back again, contemplating.

Just then, Ryan Trewet walked up. Ryan was well-dressed, in his early forties—Tim and Abigail's oldest son. The restrooms for the party guests were accessible around the side of the store building. Ryan seemed to be headed in that direction.

Ryan owned a popular fleet of speedboats on the bay in Anderson Cove that he rented out by the day and by the hour. It was big business, especially in the summertime.

"Hey, Ryan." Seth nodded politely.

Seth had met Ryan a few years ago and had caught up with him earlier this evening. He said he was looking for somewhere to hold his wife's fortieth birthday party next month and asked if Seth would rent out the wine-tasting room for such an occasion. Ryan was definitely not someone Seth could allow to see the drama that might unfold with Stacey.

Ryan slapped him on the back. "Hey, Seth. My father mentioned you're running the place now. Very impressive. I didn't realize that when we talked."

Seth nodded vigorously. "Yeah, I'm trying to hold it all together." *In more ways than one.*

"Good for you." Ryan looked at Stacey, who was smiling up at him. "And who's this?" He stuck out a hand. "Hi. Ryan Trewet."

Stacey smiled and held out a hand with a wrist full of bracelets. "Stacey Lochner, Seth's girlfriend."

Seth's eyes shot wide again and he ran a hand over his mouth a few times to keep himself from making an outburst.

"Really? Well, that's wonderful. It's so nice to meet you. He's been keeping you a secret, I see." Ryan punched Seth lightly on the arm. "I'm going to have to spread the word when I get back to the table."

Seth's face fell, but he recovered with a grin. "No, you don't have to—"

"Has he now?" Stacey interrupted, not allowing the comment to bother her. "Well, I just got here from California, so I'm afraid he almost forgot about me. I would love it if you'd spread the word for us." She laughed like it was an inside joke and tossed her hair. "It's so nice to meet you, Ryan."

Seth had forgotten how easily she could charm a stranger.

"Likewise." Ryan wiggled a few fingers at them. "All right, well I'll catch you two lovebirds later. I'm sure you have a lot of catching-up to do. And Seth, I'll give you a call about the barn."

"You got it, Ryan." Seth flashed a smile.

Ryan disappeared around the corner and Seth turned to Stacey, hushing his voice. "What are you doing?"

"What are you talking about?" Stacey shot back. "I'm being friendly."

"You just told him you're my girlfriend!" How could she be doing this? What part of *breaking up* did she not understand? "His parents are throwing this party. He knows everyone, so everyone's going to hear about this." He glanced around, struggling to keep his voice down.

"So? What's the big deal?" Stacey wrapped her hands around his left arm and stroked the sleeve of his dress shirt. "Wow, you look good tonight. And I am your girlfriend. It's true."

"No, it's not! Stacey, we broke up—a week ago. Don't you remember that?" Seth stared at her. "What on earth are you doing here? How did you even...?"

"I still love you, Seth." Stacey begged. "I want to make this work. We can still try, can't we?" She was making that face she always made right before she started to cry.

He could not have her break down here. But the problem wasn't just going to disappear by ignoring it, the way he'd ignored the problems in their relationship for months. Look where that had gotten him.

"Stacey, can you come with me, please? We need to talk." She nodded and he led her along the porch to the far side of the building where they'd have some privacy.

He didn't want her at the party with him, but judging by the way she was already behaving, it was probably safer if he kept her close. He wasn't sure what she might say or do if she became upset and he left her alone, either with the party guests or at his house. Wait—would she agree to go to the house and wait for him?

No way—she'd never agree to that. She'd throw a fit at him for even asking her to leave the party. Forget it. Bad idea.

Still, there were a lot of important people here tonight, too many potential business deals floating around that could affect the future of the orchard—he could not afford to leave things up to chance.

And Gia had a lot on the line, too. Her boss would be speaking with the Trewets on Monday to find out how she did running her first event solo. Stacey's mere presence was obviously upsetting her—and for good reason. She did not need for things to get worse.

Oh, my gosh, *Gia*. What would she be thinking by now?

Seth reached the side of the store with Stacey and stopped. He turned to look at her in the low light. He could hardly believe she was here. She looked as great as ever in a pretty dress and heels that accentuated her long legs and tanned skin. But he wasn't affected by her looks anymore—not even a little bit. All he could think about was how strange the situation was. She had to be *out of her mind* to have come all this way without telling him, after he'd just made it clear last week that it was over between them. It felt almost surreal.

"Okay, Stacey, listen. I've got a lot at stake here tonight. So do my parents, and quite frankly, the future of this entire farm depends on things going well tonight."

Stacey nodded begrudgingly.

"I didn't ask you to come here—quite frankly, I specifically asked you *not* to. But here you are, so we've got to figure this out and figure it out fast."

Stacey looked again like she might break into tears. "But why aren't you even happy to see me? You love surprises. I don't understand."

"Please don't cry, Stace. This is *not* cool. You had no business throwing this at me."

"Seth, that's cold. I wanted to prove a point—that I can do this. That I can be here for you. That I *want* to be here for you." She placed a hand on his tie and played with his collar, then ran her hand down his chest. "Please give me a chance."

He removed her hand. "It's not happening, Stacey."

"Why not? Come on, for old time's sake. You've got nothing to lose." She tried again, running her hand softly across his cheek and gazing into his eyes.

He pulled her hand away and looked off into the distance. He couldn't let her know about Gia—not yet. If she heard they were dating, she'd flip out and create that scene he was desperately hoping would not materialize.

"Because it's over between us. How do you not get that?"

"How can you say it's over just like that? We have a history together. You haven't even given me a chance. Why are you cutting me off like this?" A tear rolled down her cheek.

Seth sighed heavily. "It doesn't matter," he said with a weary shake of his head.

Stacey wiped her face. "There's someone else, isn't there?"

Seth looked up automatically and it registered on Stacey's face before he could play it off. *Shoot*. How could he have fallen for that?

"So there *is*. That's the only explanation that fits. I get it now." She narrowed her eyes. "So who is she? Is she here? Is she at your table?"

Seth cursed under his breath. She was going to figure it out and then unleash her wrath on Gia. Now he'd really done it. He was terrible at damage control, wasn't he? At least when it came to his own love life.

He rubbed his eyes and hid his face in his hands for a few seconds. Then he grabbed both of her hands and pulled them in under his chin. He looked into her eyes. "Stace, I need you to get it together and calm down. Don't ruin this party for me. If you still care about our history together, at all, you'll let it go."

Stacey's voice was cutthroat now. "Oh, I care—enough to figure out who she is. You've probably been cheating on me all summer, haven't you?" She pulled her hands away.

"As a matter of fact, I have not. You know I wouldn't do that."

Stacey cast her gaze to the ground and let out a heavy sigh.

She did know that, didn't she? He'd never done anything even questionable in all the time they were dating. Stacey had to believe him.

"All right, fine, but I still think there's something you're not telling me."

He had every right to move on and date other people, but there was no point in arguing that at the moment.

"Look, I'm sorry, Stacey. But you should know that I'd never do anything like that. And I'm not changing my mind about us. It's over—the sooner you accept that, the better."

Maybe she'd come to her senses if she knew there was no chance of them getting back together. And look what all of his ambiguity had resulted in. He'd better get it over with now—also, for Gia's sake. "Listen, you're not going to want to hear this, but yes, I do have feelings for someone else now. But nothing happened before we broke up—I swear."

"I knew it." She hung her head and began to breathe more rapidly.

"I'm sorry."

She paced for a few steps then finally took another deep breath and straightened her shoulders. "I *thought* that might be the case—all these weeks I've been trying to guess what was going on, why you broke up with me. I can't say I'm surprised."

Seth clenched his jaw. "That's not even why I broke up with you."

"Who is she? Seriously, I need to know."

"No, you don't." Seth shook his head. She wasn't going to listen to him, was she?

Stacey fumed silently.

Seth scrubbed a hand over his face again and looked at his watch. "Look, I need to get back out there." He brought his tone back down. "We can talk more later, but do you think you can just stay calm and not cause a scene? You can come and sit with me and my parents if you'll promise me that."

She could take his seat and he could mingle with the

guests at the other tables—play host. He needed to do that anyway. Dinner was almost over. His mother would help.

Stacey's face brightened a little. "Okay. Fine."

"All right, come on." It was the only way he could imagine she wouldn't wreak havoc on the evening. "But don't introduce yourself as my girlfriend to anyone else."

Stacey rolled her eyes and followed him. "Fine."

SEVENTEEN

Gia gazed at herself in the mirror of the ladies room. Her makeup still held, apart from her lipstick. But the shock on her face was going to be difficult to cover up.

She shouldn't stay there for long, but she needed a moment to collect herself. She reapplied her pink lipstick and took a deep breath. How could this be happening? Didn't he just break up with that girl? What kind of a person would fly halfway across the country, unannounced, to arrive at an ex-boyfriend's house in the middle of the countryside, with nowhere else to go if things didn't go well?

What was Stacey expecting? For him to take her back into his arms and act like nothing happened? Like everything was fine—like they hadn't just broken up? What was wrong with her?

Gia shook off the thoughts. She couldn't let the situation bother her—not tonight. There were more important things at stake, and though she'd be lying if she said she wasn't at all worried about Stacey showing up, she trusted Seth. Still, all of this was not going to be easy to ignore. She took another deep breath and marched outside.

The band had taken the stage, and the dinner plates were being swept away by an efficient catering staff. Gia sighed with relief. At least everything was going well with the party.

She would check on dessert. Abigail had chosen to go with a two-tiered vanilla cake in white frosting with gold-frosting accents. A large number 50 covered in edible glitter shimmered from the top of the second tier. It was beautiful and on display on the far side of the dance floor. Gia made her way around the back rather than cross the banquet lawn.

The photographer was already taking pictures of Abigail and Tim in front of the cake. Gia smiled. The caterers would begin cutting it and delivering slices to the tables soon. She smiled with relief at the size of it—there was plenty to go around. No counting errors had been made tonight. Thank goodness for small favors.

Gia looked away from the cake and glanced across the lawn, startled to see Seth from afar, walking back to his table—arm-in-arm with Stacey.

That was odd. A sinking sensation filled her stomach. What was going on?

She looked back at the happy couple celebrating their fifty years. How had they done it? Gia took a deep breath and glanced back at Seth. He and Stacey had reached his table, and it looked as though Stacey was going to sit in his seat. He stood behind her, talking to a member of the wait-staff, probably asking them to bring her a meal.

He'd invited her to the party? Gia huffed and then scolded herself. What else was he supposed to do with her? As long as he kept her under control, that was fine. She didn't have time for an emotional response right now. She'd just have to trust him.

She turned on her heels and headed to the catering tent for a quick check on things.

SETH PULLED up another chair at his parents' table and sat down next to Stacey, who had thrown her overnight bag at her feet under the table. Seth's mother appeared to be in as much shock as Gia had been. She tried making conversation across the table with Stacey to compensate for the awkwardness thrust upon the other guests at the table. Seth had introduced her as a friend that had just flown in for the party. His mother was doing her best to normalize the situation.

"So how are things at the Henderson Estates, Stacey?"

Stacey downed the last drops of the glass of champagne that had been intended for Seth for the toast earlier—which he'd missed—and looked over at his mom. "Thanks for asking," she said flippantly, "but I don't know. I quit."

Seth's jaw dropped, but he recovered before anyone besides his parents noticed. His mouth gaped open. Not only was Stacey being rude to his guests, but she'd quit her job? How permanent an arrangement did she really think she'd find here? She really believed she was staying here and that he'd still give her the job he'd promised her two months ago?

Or was she just yanking his chain? She knew how to get a rise out of him—this little story was certainly working. Maybe it wasn't true. He'd play along.

"You quit?" his mother repeated, looking baffled. "Well, that's a—surprise."

"Seth already hired me, so it wasn't as though I left a job without lining up another one first."

It was his father's turn to sit back with his eyes nearly popping out of their sockets. "I thought we...?" He directed his gaze at Seth.

Seth shot his dad a look and shook his head. *Please don't.* His father went silent and stabbed his fork into a piece of asparagus.

"Excuse me, is there a bar here somewhere so I can get another drink?" Stacey asked the woman sitting to her left.

"Yes, it's right over there," the woman answered politely, pointing.

Seth took a quick look around. People had started leaving the dinner tables and streaming out onto the dance floor. The bar area was filling up again with people who stood around chatting and laughing. Stacey's plate of food hadn't arrived yet.

"Great. I'll be right back then."

Seth spoke under his breath. "Don't you think you should slow down?"

Stacey pushed her chair back and stood up, grabbing her handbag. "Nope," she said at full volume. "I don't." She tossed her hair and walked off. So much for his plan. His mother wasn't going to be able to handle Stacey. She would have to be his problem tonight.

Seth stood and followed her, but he was quickly intercepted by the older couple who owned the apple orchard just down the road from the Pederson's property. They'd been seated at the next table. "Oh, Seth, I'm glad I caught you!" Mr. Adams grabbed his arm. "We've been eager to see you. You're so grown up!"

Seth greeted them, trying to keep Stacey in his sights, but she'd already left him far behind. He watched from the corner of his eye as she reached the bar. The last thing she needed were too many drinks. At best, she'd become unpredictable, and at worst, she'd become a powder keg. Tonight was definitely looking like a worst-case scenario—scorned ex-girlfriend, determined to have her way. He needed to get to her fast.

"Thanks so much, Mr. and Mrs. Adams. It's great to see you. But hey, I've got to head over…" He looked at the bar again. She was ordering already. "Let me catch up with you in a bit, okay?" He laid a hand over Mr. Adams' shoulder as the man nodded agreeably. Seth hurried off.

He reached Stacey just as she threw back a shot of whiskey. She made a face to shake off the slow burn of the alcohol. "Whew! That was fun! You want one?" she said.

"No, I don't," Seth answered with irritation. "Stace, you said you were going to stay calm tonight."

"I am calm. Look at me. You're the one who needs to relax." She turned to the bartender and ordered a glass of red wine. "Whatever you've got is fine."

"You haven't even eaten yet. You need to slow down."

"Uh, you're not my boyfriend anymore, apparently, so you have *no say* in anything I do. Remember?"

Uh-oh.

"And this is a party. You should lighten up." She rolled her eyes. "What happened to you, Seth? You used to be so much fun." Her glass of red wine arrived and she thanked the bartender and took a sip. "I guess you're right. This place has changed you." She sauntered away from Seth and stopped at the edge of the bar area to look around.

It was an open bar, but Seth dropped a few dollars in front of the bartender since Stacey hadn't bothered to tip him. "Please don't serve her anything else," he said so Stacey couldn't hear.

The bartender nodded.

Seth caught up to Stacey and slipped his arms gently

around her waist. It was time to step up the damage control. He led her back toward the table. "All right, I'll relax and try to have fun. But you take it easy too, okay?" He meant on the alcohol, but frankly, he was a little too scared to say the words. She might bite off his tongue if he did. She was already buzzed.

She ignored the question. "So can you call me a cab later? I'll go back to my new apartment. I thought I was going to be able to stay at your house tonight, but now, I guess that's not happening." She pushed some hair behind her ear and shot him a defiant look.

Seth's eyes shot wide. "Your what?" It was loud now because of the music playing, but Seth was pretty sure he'd heard her right. *Please don't say you rented the apartment.*

"My new place. I took that apartment you went and saw in Heritage Bay, after all. Sent in my security deposit this week. Got the key tonight. Dropped off my suitcases before I came here."

"You've got to be kidding me!" Seth stopped and looked her in the eye. How could she have gone through with all of this after their conversation last week? He clenched a fist and kept walking.

Several moments later, they sat back down at the table. Stacey's food had arrived. She pulled it in front of her and nibbled on a few bites then took another substantial gulp of her wine.

Seth took in a deep breath and finished what was left of the now-warm lager he'd been enjoying before the craziness had set in.

He was *this* close to creating a scene of his own right there if she didn't settle down.

Dessert had been passed around to some of the tables already. Seth's mother pushed aside her empty cake plate and dabbed at her face with her cloth napkin. "So, Stacey, how does your family feel about you coming to Wisconsin to take a new job? Were they sorry to see you leave?"

Stacey pursed her lips. "Yes," Stacey said. "As a matter of fact, they were very upset with me." It seemed she was no longer trying to impress his parents like she had over the video chat.

"Oh." His mother obviously had not expected such a direct response.

Seth raised his brow at his mother and she shot him a look—*I give up*.

He could see why his mother would feel that way. Stacey had resorted to shock value, and it was all to try to get back at him. He was in for a ride, wasn't he? She'd only just gotten started.

Stacey stood up abruptly. "I'm going to dance. Who wants to dance?" She looked around the table. Most of the couples there were his parents' age. They might dance tonight, but not with an obnoxious twenty-something. They shook their heads or smiled politely without answering. One of the women shot a reproachful look at his mother, shaking her head.

Stacey downed the last of her wine and marched off. Seth glanced at his mother and jumped up to follow her, mouthing the word to his mother. *Sorry*.

GIA CAUGHT Seth's eye as he marched behind Stacey. Seth shot her a look with a shake of his head. *Don't ask*. He kept moving.

A waiter passed them with glasses of white wine on a tray and Stacey took one, although it looked as though Seth said something to her when she did. Seth took one for himself as the waiter was walking off and threw back a long swig. He looked livid.

Uh-oh. That wasn't like Seth. What was going on?

She watched as Stacey pulled him out onto the dance floor and began to shake to the beat. It was a fast, popular song from the early 2000s, and Gia laughed nervously as Seth tried to keep up with Stacey. He laughed and started to dance and Gia covered her mouth and looked away because it was turning her stomach to see him out there with her.

This was the girl Seth used to have real feelings for. What if Stacey reminded him why he used to love her? What if she convinced him to take her back tonight? Gia turned and walked away. She couldn't watch.

An hour later, the sun had gone down and the tiny white lights strung from the trees lent a hint of enchantment to the evening. Gia did a quick lap around the party, scanning the crowd. It looked as though most people were enjoying themselves. She saw Tim and Abigail mingling near the bar with more of their guests, all of whom seemed lost in discussion or storytelling.

So far, so good. Fifteen minutes later, she ended up back at the dance floor where most of the action was now focused.

The music changed to a softer melody from the 1990s. Gia knew the song well. It was a love song, one of her favorites from that era, still regularly played on the radio. The cover band was doing a great job tonight. She made a note to let Noreen know. Her boss always liked to know which bands were crowd-pleasers.

Gia stopped to listen to the song, wishing like crazy that Stacey hadn't shown up tonight. Gia would be swaying to the music, her arms wrapped around Seth right now if she hadn't.

Gia raised an eyebrow as Seth tried to leave the dance floor, urging Stacey to follow him. He locked eyes with Gia for a quick second and she smiled supportively. He returned an affectionate glance. She scrunched up her nose and gave him a knowing look. *Miss you.* At least he wasn't going to slow-dance with Stacey. Thank heavens for small favors.

In the next moment, Seth's attention was drawn back to Stacey as she refused to leave, dragging him back out onto the dance floor. Gia's expression changed as she watched him shake his head at her. The crowd thinned around them to give them space over their apparent lovers' quarrel, and Seth must've noticed the looks they were getting. Two seconds later, Stacey had folded her hands together behind his neck and pulled herself in close to him. She rested her head against his chin and they moved to the music.

Gia watched, her smile gone. She felt her pulse in her throat as Seth locked his hands behind Stacey's back. It looked like a comfortable, old habit for them. Gia swallowed, folded her arms, lowered her chin, and walked away.

That should have been her.

How was she going to get the image of them, locked in an embrace, out of her head?

EIGHTEEN

Seth closed his eyes, his arms around Stacey, and let out a sigh. Could tonight be any more awkward and ridiculous? He had done everything in his power to break off their relationship—but here he was, forced to slow dance with the woman who was intentionally wreaking havoc on his business and personal life.

He longed to be holding Gia out here under the soft lights, swaying to the beat without a care in the world but the feel of her cheek against his, his arms around her. He'd promised her a dance, but that dance would have to wait. He only hoped she understood what was going on tonight, and that she'd even grant him that chance again in the future. He had to talk to her soon, even if he only had time to make sure she wasn't upset. He could tell her everything else later tonight.

He looked at his watch over Stacey's shoulder. The party was almost over. He'd barely had a chance to drum up any more business with any of these well-connected people regarding the venue spaces, either. He still needed to rub elbows with some of them before he missed his chance.

The song ended and he took Stacey's hand and pulled her gently off the dance floor. He was pretty sure she'd keep it together in front of other well-meaning, well-dressed strangers who weren't associated with his family, the same way she'd behaved pleasantly with Ryan Trewet. It was time to find out. "Come on. Let's go talk to some of my friends."

GIA WAS TRYING to stay out of the way and keep an eye on the party from various vantage points. Seth and Stacey had left the dance floor a while back, and Gia couldn't see them from where she'd situated herself next to the flowering arbor at the far end of the banquet lawn.

She gazed at the climbing roses then checked her watch. Nine thirty. In about another hour, the party would be over, and, about half an hour after that, she could call it a night. The catering staff would make sure that everything was cleaned up and put back where it belonged. The band would take down all of its own equipment and load it up themselves. The supply company would return and cart away the tables and chairs along with everything else. By the time they all rolled out of there, it would look like no party had even taken place. All she'd have left to do this evening was pay the balances on the vendors' bills.

She sighed, hoping her relief wouldn't be premature. A lot could still go wrong in an hour. Seth has been doing a great job keeping his unpredictable ex-girlfriend under control, however. At least there was that. She fought back a yawn. It had also been a long day.

"Hey."

Startled, she turned at the sound of Seth's voice. She relaxed.

He smiled apologetically and moved in close. "Listen, Gia, I am beyond sorry about all of this. I don't trust her enough to leave her alone for very long." His eyes said it all. "That's why you haven't seen much of me tonight."

Gia eyed him. He looked tired. She guessed Stacey had put him through the wringer. "It's okay. I get it, and believe me, I appreciate it. Where is she now?"

"I left her with a couple of single guys I know from high school. They're fawning all over her. Should help with the bruised ego."

That was smart.

He fought off the look of exasperation. "I might have signed up another couple of clients who want the winery space for a party, too, by the way. I'll give them your office number when I follow up with them this week."

"Oh, that's great!" She smiled and he seemed to relax.

He shook his head again, though. "Oh hey, so she's totally drunk. I don't know what might happen to her if I were to send her somewhere in a cab. Are you okay with it if she stays in my parents' guest room? I don't really think I need to say this to you, but I will say it anyway—nothing will happen. I promise you."

Gia had expected this to happen, but she didn't have to like it. "Of course. I trust you. Do what you need to do."

"Thanks." Seth smiled and grabbed her hand in a way that wouldn't be noticeable to passersby. He squeezed it and she softly stroked the back of his hand with her thumb.

"Well, hey, I just wanted to check in with you for a minute before I get back to babysitting." He dropped her hand. "Everything seems to be going well—outside of this drama, right? It's been hard for me to tell."

"I can imagine. But, yeah. The party's been great." She crossed two fingers and held them up. "We're almost to the finish line."

Seth nodded. "Thank goodness." He turned to look at her again. "Oh hey, look, one more thing. Stacey can't know about you—at least not tonight."

"I kind of figured that when I saw you dancing with her," Gia said dryly. "But why? What's she been saying?"

"I'm sorry about that, too." He frowned. "She figured it out early on that I'm seeing someone, so I fessed up and told her she was right. Anyway, now she's trying to figure out who it is. If she does, she'll throw a fit. Worse than the one she's already been throwing." He smiled at a young couple that strolled by, nodding to make it look like he wasn't discussing anything unusual.

Gia furrowed her brow. "Oh. Okay." She let out a frustrated sigh.

Seth nodded. "I'm really sorry about all this." He stroked her elbow.

She had to just let it go. Deep breath. Eyes on the prize.

"I know." Gia had to give him credit—he was trying to make her feel better. Maybe there were no old feelings that had been revived in his heart tonight for Stacey. She probably shouldn't have let her mind go there. "As long as this party goes off without a hitch—whatever it takes, I guess."

"My thoughts exactly." He sounded anxious. "Please don't be mad."

She nodded. "I'm not mad. It's okay. Go ahead back to your guests. I'll be fine."

He glanced around then leaned back in and stole a quick kiss. "That's for now, but there's more for later," he said, grinning.

Well, maybe not later, because Stacey would be with him later, but—eventually. In a few days, maybe?

Gia forced a smile. Still, he was right. This weird little charade would be over with soon. The party was the most important thing tonight, not her love life. She'd just have to keep reminding herself of that until it was over.

Seth turned to leave and almost walked right into one of the party guests. The man looked to be in his early forties, good-looking, wearing an expensive suit.

The man stepped back, glanced at Gia curiously from several feet away, then gave Seth a once-over. "Oh hey, man. Sorry."

Was this Abigail's oldest son? Gia thought he looked familiar. He seemed to have had several drinks.

"Ryan! Good to see you again. Making the rounds?" Seth asked.

Was that a note of concern in Seth's voice? And, yes, that was it—*Ryan Trewet*, Tim and Abigail's oldest.

"Sure am. And I see *you're* making the rounds, too." He cocked a brow. "Where's your, uh, girlfriend from earlier? She was really cute." He socked Seth playfully on the arm.

What was going on here?

Seth still looked worried. "Uh, nah, that wasn't actually—"

Ryan looked confused.

Seth cleared his throat and took a few steps back toward Gia. "Ryan, this is Gia Stewart. She's my girlfriend."

Gia smiled and said hello just as Stacey sauntered up. It appeared as though she hadn't heard the exchange. "There you are, Seth! I've been looking all over for you." She carried a glass of white wine, half finished, and she looked as though she'd had several others tonight. She turned with a flirtatious look. "Oh, hi, Ryan! It's great to see you again!"

Gia glanced from Seth to Stacey to Ryan. She should steal away—now. Something wasn't right.

Ryan cleared his throat. "Well, hello there, Ms. Cali-forn-i-ay." He shot a look at Gia and back at Seth. "Okay, I'll just stay out of it," he muttered, turning.

"Stay out of what?" Stacey asked, sounding innocent. She looked at Seth, who glanced back at Ryan then quickly looked away.

"Oh, nothing. Sorry, didn't mean to intrude." Ryan looked at Gia one more time then turned on his heels and left.

Stacey let her glance fall on Gia.

Gia raised her eyebrows. "Hi Stacey. How's your evening going?" she ventured. *Careful, now.*

Stacey narrowed her eyes at Seth. "What was Ryan intruding on?" She turned back to glare at Gia.

Seth shoved a hand in the pocket of his suit pants. "Nothing. Gia's coordinating the event tonight. I was just checking in with her to make sure everything's been running smoothly."

Gia nodded, maybe a little too eagerly. Was she buying it? "That's right." She cleared her throat as Stacey's expression grew more concerned. "And things are going just fine," Gia continued. "I'll be on my way now. I'll check in with you later, Seth." She slipped past Stacey to leave.

Stacey eyeballed Seth. "It's *her*, isn't it?" she hissed.

Gia caught her breath and looked back. Stacey sized up Gia. "She's the new girlfriend, isn't she?"

Gia's eyes flew wide. She looked to Seth. *Now what?*

"It all makes perfect sense. You two have been working on this for weeks together, haven't you?" She glared at Seth. "That's why you've been so excited about throwing this rager." Her tone was full of sarcasm.

And rage.

Seth took Stacey gently by the arm. "That's enough, Stace."

She shook free of him. "Like I said—you don't get to tell me what to do."

"I never *have* told you what to do." His voice was icy. "Stacey, I'm *asking* you not to make a scene tonight. Can you please just—"

"What's the matter? You don't like being called out as a two-timer?"

Gia really wanted to walk away, but she couldn't just stand by and let the situation get out of control. Her entire professional reputation was at risk. This monster was going to make a huge scene if they didn't calm her down, and it was Gia's job to put out sparks like this before they became full-blown fires.

She stepped forward. "Look, Stacey, nobody's been two-timing anyone. This is a big misunderstanding. If you'll just take a moment to—"

"—That's exactly what I'd expect you to say, blondie." She returned her gaze to Seth. "So how long has this been going on?"

Seth glared at her. "Nothing's going on here—except for you making accusations."

"Which are all true," Stacey shot back.

"Stacey!" Seth's voice was loud. Gia could tell he was about to lose it.

"Seth, don't let her do this to you."

Stacey smiled devilishly. "Go on, listen to your new girlfriend," she said, pretending to pout. "She knows what to do. She's in *charge* here."

Seth's nostrils flared. He drew in a heavy breath and let it out.

Gia looked beyond him. A small crowd of curious partygoers had stopped to watch. *Oh, for crying out loud.* It was happening—the scene.

"Stacey, please..." Gia mustered as calmly as she could. "Come with me and I'll get you something to—"

Stacey edged a few steps closer to Gia. "Look at her. Long blonde hair. Perfect blue eyes. *Pretty in pink.* How predictable." She looked disgusted. "I thought you had more sophisticated taste than *this*." She took a few locks of Gia's wavy blonde hair and yanked.

"Ouch!" Gia cried.

Stacey let go and Gia took a step back, stunned. Ouch. *Now what?*

Did that seriously just happen?

"How dare you?" Seth grabbed Stacey by the hand and marched her away.

Tim and Ryan Trewet stepped through the group of onlookers, their eyes bulging, as Seth and Stacey hurried off in the dark, toward the farmhouse.

"What in the world happened here?" Tim said, alarmed. He must've seen the exchange from a distance. Gia gaped at him, her gut clenching.

Abigail showed up behind them a moment later, and her face said it all. *What have you done?*

SETH SAT with his mother in the kitchen under a low light. His father had gone to bed. Stacey had passed out in their guest room half an hour ago, after a long and agonizing discussion—or was it just an argument?—about how things were never going to work out between them. How circumstances and geography had played a role but that his feelings for her were gone. There was nothing he could do about it. Coming back to Wisconsin had changed everything, and there was no going back to what they used to have together.

Stacey had shed a lot of tears but drank a lot of water and had taken a few aspirin before she passed out. Seth hoped the hangover wouldn't be too rough tomorrow.

She finally believed him when he said he didn't cheat on her with Gia, but she still didn't like it that he was already seeing someone only three weeks after they'd broken up.

He understood. He might've felt the same way if things had been reversed, although he wouldn't have flown across the country to try to change her mind.

Whatever the case, she'd be more like herself tomorrow. *Let's hope.* He shook his glass and threw back some of the ice cubes from the bottom of his ice water.

"So Mom," he said quietly, "I'm really sorry about all this. I know tonight was very important to the future of the farm. I'll call the Trewets tomorrow and apologize."

"Thanks, honey, but I'm more concerned about Gia. I hope they don't speak badly of her." His mother sipped a cup of cider. "After all, the party was beautiful and she ran it well. The agency did a wonderful job and I don't think we scared off any potential customers because of one little lovers' quarrel. But Gia doesn't deserve to take the blame for this from her superiors."

Seth nodded. He agreed wholeheartedly. *He* deserved to take the blame.

"And I don't think anyone, except maybe Abigail, was actually upset by the incident tonight, and she'll come around. That woman was full of drama when she was young." His mother smiled, remembering the good old days.

"Oh, if she didn't play the field in high school. That woman broke more hearts than I've broken dishes in my lifetime."

Seth chuckled. "Well, that's a surprise. Maybe she'll go easy on her, then."

"I hope so." His mother took another sip of the cider.

He stood up. "Well, hey, I'm going to try to call Gia now." He picked up his phone from the table and gave his mother a kiss on the forehead. She reached out and wrapped an arm around his waist and held him there. "If I'd have known you were such a heartbreaker, yourself, I'd have told you what you were doing wrong, honey. Next time, tell me what's going on before you go and make a mess of it. I'm here to help." She smiled.

Seth laughed. He'd remember that. She'd already saved him once. "All right, Mom. I will."

NINETEEN

Gia parked in the usual spot outside her apartment building and turned off the lights. She climbed out of the car and trudged up the stairs to her front door in the dark. She checked her watch. Almost midnight.

Inside the apartment, she dropped her things on the counter and poured a glass of ice water, then sucked it down and refilled the glass.

What a night. She shook her head. Chaos. A cat fight, as it was probably being called by some of the party guests by now. What if someone had filmed it on a phone? *Oh no. Please, no.*

She closed her eyes and took a deep breath. *Let it go.*

What would Stacey be doing by now? Probably sleeping off the alcohol—with any luck. Hopefully, Seth would be asleep by now, too.

Gia jumped as her phone rang and Seth's name lit up the screen. She reached to pick it up and then slowly pulled her hand back. Was she really ready to talk about this debacle with him right now? She listened to it ring again, watched it light up once more. No, she wasn't.

What could she possibly say to him right now? The whole thing had been just a bit too over-the-top. She was humiliated, frustrated, angry, and worried about her job, to boot. It would be better to wait until tomorrow before they talked. It wouldn't help to say something she'd regret.

He'd probably be exhausted, anyway, and assume she was asleep. She walked into the living area and plopped down on her couch, setting the phone on the coffee table.

Would she still even have a job on Monday? To handle an incident like the one tonight was not unheard of at weddings and parties. But to be at the center of the controversy—that was something else entirely.

Abigail would surely call Noreen tomorrow, or Monday, perhaps, and tell her what had happened. So Gia would have to get out in front of it and catch Noreen *before* that happened. She'd call her first thing in the morning and explain. Noreen frequently worked on Sundays, after all.

Still, the whole thing made her uneasy. Queasy, even. She stared at the coffee table in front of her.

She'd tried so hard to make tonight a success. She'd given it everything she had, all month. Noreen was dangling it over her head like a carrot to a horse. All Gia'd had to do was pull the cart and get the job done. The step up at the agency had been right there in front of her, all month, but now, it was, once again, out of reach.

It was so unfair that this stubborn, irrational, vengeful excuse for a woman could unravel it with a temper tantrum. Stacey was unbelievable. How could Seth have dated her for so long?

Still, she felt sorry for Seth. He'd done his best tonight to keep Stacey under control—for hours. It was his feelings for Gia that had been their undoing. He'd come over to reassure her—sweet man that he was—and then he'd let his emotions get the best of him. That kiss—Ryan Trewet never would've suspected a thing if Seth hadn't kissed her. Still, Gia had appreciated it. It had almost neutralized the torture of watching him slow dance with his ex-girlfriend. He'd only been trying to make her feel better.

Gia's eyes felt moist. She sighed heavily and let out a short sob. What a mess.

She sat back and began to skim through her messages, and Tom's name popped up. *That's right.* He'd called earlier. He'd probably love this story. It would just prove his assumptions—that Seth was trouble.

Oh well, he had a point—on some level.

It was Saturday night, around midnight, and Tom was probably out with their friends. Now was as good a time as any to try him back. Even if he did feel the need to preach at her first, he'd be willing to lend an ear.

She ran a finger over Tom's name on her phone.

Tom picked up on the second ring. "Gia! This is a surprise. Whatcha doin'?"

She sniffled. "Just got home from the anniversary party." She wiped her nose. "I saw you called earlier."

"Oh, right. Hey, one sec. I'm at the bar and it's loud. Let me go outside." About fifteen seconds passed while Gia heard music and voices on the other end of the line. "Okay, I can hear you now," he said. "So you said you just got home from the party—how'd it go?"

Gia leaned her head to one side. "It was all right." She went quiet.

"All right? What's wrong, honey?"

Gia sighed heavily. "It was good. It just all fell apart at the end."

"What did?"

Gia thought she might burst into tears. *Don't be so*

dramatic. Hold it together, Stewart. "Just—everything." She swallowed, shook off the feeling, and drank more of her ice water. That was better.

"Everything? Well, gosh, that sounds like a horrible party."

Gia laughed.

"Are you sure you should be doing this for a living? I mean—event planners are supposed to throw parties that stay together at the end."

She laughed again. He could always do that for her. She sighed. "You know that time you offered to come over and make me feel better and I told you I'd take a rain check?"

"Of course I do." Tom sounded more serious.

Gia was quiet again for a few seconds before she spoke. "Can I cash in that rain check now?"

"Absolutely, sweetie. I'll be right over."

Gia changed into sweats and a T-shirt and twenty minutes later, Tom was at her door. She let him in with a short hug and they stood in her living room. He seemed to have had a few drinks. But then again, he'd been at the local watering hole. Gia didn't mind.

"Nick dropped me off. He and Courtney were just leaving the bar, anyway."

"Aw, that was nice of them."

She'd tell Courtney and Kira about this tomorrow—they'd want to hear about it.

He set his phone down on the table by the door.

Gia nodded. "Thanks for coming over." She put her hands on her hips and made a pouty face.

Tom gazed at her. "You look like you need a real hug."

Gia looked at him. "That's because I do."

Tom reached out and wrapped her in a bear hug.

Finally, he pulled back. "So what happened? Start at the beginning."

They settled in on the couch together.

Gia explained about the party, how well it had gone, and how Stacey had shown up unannounced. And then how things had gone downhill from there.

Tom sat back. "Wow. What a night."

"So isn't this the part where you tell me how awful Seth is?"

Tom shook his head. "Nope. Not really. I mean, I'm sure he could've done a few things differently, but sounds like he made the best of a lousy situation."

Well that was a surprise. Gia nodded. She felt a lot better having talked it all through. "Okay, well good. Thanks for listening, sweetie. I'm so lucky to have you as a friend."

He reached out and pulled her closer to him on the couch so her head rested on his shoulder. He put his arm around her casually. Still, it was just a friendly embrace.

"So, what's going on with you and Seth then? Why didn't you call *him* tonight? Besides the fact that his extremely territorial ex-girlfriend is having a sleepover at his house?"

Gia laughed. "Oh, right. *That*."

"Yeah, that." Tom grinned.

"I needed a breather, I guess. It was a lot to take, and I feel like if he'd have handled this breakup differently in the first place, she might never have shown up here at all. Do you think so? Or am I way off?"

Tom nodded. "I have to agree with you there. He probably could've handled things differently."

"I mean, what if he's like this with me six months down the road if things aren't working out between us? As badly as this girl behaved tonight, I couldn't help but feel for her on some level. I imagine Seth would be a difficult guy to lose."

"But I can't see you losing your mind like that and pulling some girl's ponytail."

Gia laughed. "True. That's just not my style."

Tom nodded, but stayed quiet for a bit. Finally, he cleared his throat. "Gia, when I called you earlier tonight, I was trying to get through so I could warn you."

"What?" Gia's brow tightened and she sat up. "Warn me? About what?"

Tom took a deep breath and let it out. "Stacey rented an apartment at my complex today. She took the key this afternoon. Apparently, she signed the lease a few days ago, and I saw it, but I didn't put two and two together and realize who she was—until she showed up today."

Gia sat up and stared at him. "She rented an apartment here?"

Tom nodded.

She considered it for a few seconds, her thoughts racing. "That's unbelievable. But, how did you know who she was? Was she walking around telling perfect strangers about her and Seth or something?"

Tom cast his gaze across the room and then looked back at her. He shook his head. "No. But I have a confession to make."

Gia's face fell. She lowered her voice. "What are you talking about?"

Tom looked her in the eye. "Okay. Seth came and looked at the apartment for her a few weeks ago, like, well over a week before the bonfire. I showed him the unit. He told me his name, and you had just told us about him at the diner that week, so it clicked for me who he was. And when

I asked, he said the place wasn't for him—it was for his girlfriend..." Tom looked at the floor. "From California."

Gia's eyes went wide. She shook her head emphatically. "That can't be right." She crossed her arms. "He said he wanted to leave her for weeks before he met me. Why wouldn't he tell me this?"

"Gia, apparently she told our receptionist that she had a job lined up already, too—at the Pederson Winery."

Gia sat back. "A job? Oh, my gosh."

She stood up and started pacing in front of the coffee table, distraught. "But how—why...? And how could he check out an apartment for her and never even tell me she'd been planning to move here?" This was much more serious than he'd let on. "He was going to give her a job, really?"

"And apparently, she still thinks he is." Tom sighed.

"Well, maybe not after tonight." Gia cocked a brow.

Did she?

There's no way.

But still.

How could he have left out such important details about Stacey? Things between them had obviously been much more serious than he'd even let on.

Gia's stomach started to turn again.

She leaned forward on the couch and ran her hands through her hair. Then again, he'd explained *some* of this. He had told Gia it had been serious. Maybe Seth had figured she'd realize the apartment and the job were no longer happening when they broke up and never thought Stacey would think otherwise? Maybe he thought it was water under the bridge. That *had* to be it.

Still, why hadn't he told Gia about all this? She'd asked him specifically to be up front with her. He'd said he would.

Gia's cheeks felt warm. She stared at Tom. "But wait,

Tom—you knew about this and you didn't tell me, either." She raised her voice a notch. "Why didn't you tell me?"

Tom scratched his head. "I know. And I'm sorry. But honestly, I was trying to protect you." He turned up his mouth on one side. "There was no certainty in it at that point—she hadn't actually rented the place yet—and then you told me a few weeks later that Seth broke up with her, so I figured it was over and done with." He stopped to study Gia's face. "But then, out of nowhere, she showed up today. Someone else in the office processed the paperwork for her this week. I only realized who she was when she walked into the office with a couple of suitcases to pick up her key, and she gave me her name. I asked her what had brought her to Heritage Bay and she told me. I called you as soon as she left."

Gia cupped a hand across her mouth. She sat back down on the couch and pulled her feet underneath her legs. "I'm sorry I didn't take your call." She cast a shadowed look at Tom. "But I really wish you'd have told me before. Maybe some of this craziness would never have happened if I'd have known because I would've confronted Seth with it, way before any of this could happen." Gia crossed her arms over her chest. "Or at least I'd have known what I was getting myself into."

Tom blew out a breath. "I wish I had, too."

Gia huffed. Now she was angry with both of the men in her life.

Tom sat forward on the couch. "Maybe I should go."

"I think that would be best." Her voice was still harsh. She stared at the carpet. "I need to be alone." Her thoughts still churned, but she no longer wanted to talk.

Tom nodded, stood up, and went to grab his phone on the other end of the room. He pulled up the app and called a ride. "It says the guy'll be here in five minutes. I'll wait outside." He opened the door to leave and looked back. "I'm sorry, Gia."

This was not how she'd expected this night to go down—not at all. She looked up. "Wait." She stood up and hurried over then hugged him. "I'm sorry, too. Thanks for looking out for me."

"Well, I kinda failed at that, but..."

She shook her head. "No, you didn't. It's okay."

He squeezed her tight and held her there for several moments before he pulled back. "Get some rest. You guys'll figure it out."

Gia nodded and Tom headed downstairs.

SUNDAY MORNING ARRIVED, and Seth was out of the house early. It seemed that everything from the party had been cleaned up well, so he'd taken care of a few things in the orchard and then stopped in at the office to do an hour's worth of bookkeeping.

Stacey hadn't been up yet when he'd left to check on the property, but his mother said she'd deal with her. She'd be making breakfast. A good meal, some coffee, an ounce of patience, and an ounce of understanding ought to help move things along today. His mother's words.

He'd tried calling Gia but she hadn't answered, and she hadn't returned either of his calls. He'd sent a text but hadn't heard back yet, either. It was unusual for her. She must be really upset. One thing at a time, though. He could hardly blame her.

He'd phoned Abigail Trewet and apologized profusely—his mother had her number. He took full blame for the undignified behavior on display by his ex-girlfriend and himself. He explained the unusual circumstances and what had transpired between Ryan and him and between the women, leaving out the seedier details, but he'd been sure to mention that Gia and the Jenkins Agency had nothing to do with it. Abigail assured him that she would take that into account when she spoke to Noreen. Seth had thanked her for understanding.

Around eleven, Seth came back to the farmhouse to find that Stacey had showered, dressed, and eaten. She sat at the kitchen table talking over coffee with his mother, and they both looked up and greeted him when he walked into the room. His mother smiled but Stacey looked worried.

"Well, well, what do we have here?" he asked pleasantly.

His mother answered for them. "We did the dishes. We were just having a nice chat."

Seth poured himself some coffee and joined them at the table.

"It seems Stacey has some great stories about you and all of your friends in Sonoma. I was enjoying hearing about your last few years there—when I never got to see you."

Seth felt a guilty pang for having been gone for so many years. He rested an arm on the table and forced a grin. "Ah. All good stories I hope?"

Stacey returned the look. "Give or take a few."

His mother set down her coffee cup and wiped the corner of her lip. "One in particular where you happened to drop an entire bottle of expensive red wine all over the floor in front of a roomful of customers."

"Ouch." Seth nodded sheepishly and Stacey grinned again.

"Sorry. I couldn't help myself," she confessed.

Seth laughed. "Not one of my proudest moments. That one came out of my paycheck."

His mother grinned. "I'll bet it did."

Seth's father came into the room and sat down at the table. "Stacey's been telling us you did some great work at the Henderson Estates, son. She said when you were managing the place, revenues increased by twenty percent the first month."

Seth smiled. That was true. It seemed that Stacey was, indeed, back on her best behavior. He sighed with relief and shot her a friendly look.

"Yeah, I made some changes when I started and got lucky—they worked."

"Oh, he's always so modest." His mom scolded him. But she was beaming; he knew she wouldn't have it any other way. "Seth, why don't you take Stacey out and show her the orchard and the barn? She didn't get a chance to see it yesterday."

Seth nodded. "That's a great idea. Let me just grab something to eat first. Any breakfast left?"

"Sure is. I made you a plate. It's waiting for you in the microwave."

He turned on the machine and swiped the panel. "Thanks, Mom."

TWENTY

Even Marcy and Angela had the whole day off, so Kira and Courtney had talked them and Gia into spending their Sunday on a four-mile hike through the shady wooded trails of nearby Headland State Park. It wasn't often the girls were all free at the same time, so they'd grabbed sandwiches and iced lattes at the West End Coffee Shop and headed out for some fresh air and exercise.

Angela led the way up a mossy hill with Courtney on her heels, and Gia brought up the middle.

"So how'd the anniversary party go last night, Gia?" Kira raised her voice from the back of the line so the others could hear.

"It went well, thanks." Gia said with forced enthusiasm as she stepped over a log in the trail. She told them about the beautiful setup, the fun cover band, and how everything had stayed on schedule.

"Sounds great!" Marcy said. "So how'd it go with you and Seth, first time working side by side? I really liked him when we talked at the bonfire, by the way. You found yourself a winner, Gia."

Should she get into it? She wasn't sure she wanted to get upset again. "Thanks, Marcy. And actually, no problems on that front. He's really good at working a room. Total social butterfly. He was in his element."

"Did you get to dance with him?" Courtney asked. "It sounds like it was so romantic."

If only she knew. "It really was. The orchard looked amazing all dressed up..." She paused. "But no. We were going to..." Gia hesitated and let out a heavy sigh. "Okay, you guys, so things got a little out of control." She proceeded to tell them the whole story about Stacey, all the way through to the part where she pulled Gia's hair and accused Seth of cheating on her.

"Get *out*!" Angela stopped to turn around and gape at Gia for a few seconds as they left the shade of the trees and started into a meadow. Tall grasses and the occasional birch tree grew on either side of the trail and wildflowers clustered randomly among the lush foliage. "She pulled your hair? What is this, second grade?" Angela let out another roar of laughter.

"I know, right?" Gia laughed and tightened her long ponytail, which hung through the opening in her baseball cap.

"I would've pulled hers back." Angela beat a fist against the palm of her other hand.

"We know you would've, Ang," Marcy said, smirking. Angela gave a firm nod of her head.

But Courtney looked concerned. "Does your boss know about it yet, Gia?"

Angela took a drink from her water bottle then turned and started walking again. They all followed suit.

"I called her this morning and explained. She was horrified, but she didn't fire me," Gia said. "Said she'll talk to the client about it before she makes any decisions, but she thanked me for bringing it to her first."

"Well, that's good, at least," Marcy offered. "You're probably fine."

"I hope so." Gia nodded. "But who knows?"

"So then what's going on with this wacky ex-girlfriend today? Did she stay at his house last night?" Kira was intrigued.

Gia nodded again. "As far as I know, yes. I don't have any more details because I'm afraid of what he'll tell me, honestly."

"Oh," Kira replied. "I get that."

"Actually, Seth called me twice since last night, but I haven't picked up," Gia admitted. "Texted me a few times, too. I keep getting the willies every time I think about him there with her. He slow danced with her—just to keep her from making a scene. She was all over him. It was hard to watch."

"Aw, but he can't honestly want to get back together with her, right?" Kira went on. "She sounds like a real piece of work."

"Fingers crossed." Gia made a face.

Courtney turned around to glance at Gia. "So are you and Seth in a fight now, or what? He's probably wondering what's going on if you're not answering his calls, right?"

What good was having a solid group of girlfriends if she didn't accept their offer to be her sounding board every now and then? She might as well tell them everything.

Gia sighed. "You're right. There's a whole other *thing* that happened." She told them about the conversation with Tom last night and how Stacey signed a lease and said that Seth gave her a job.

"What gets me is that the only thing I asked of Seth

when he finally told me about Stacey was that I needed complete honesty from him, from there on out." She motioned with her hands to emphasize. "I asked him to be completely up front, no matter what. He said he would. But then I find out about this. I don't know what to think now."

"Okay, yeah, that's huge." Marcy agreed. "He should've told you, and then none of this would've come as a surprise."

"Exactly." Gia frowned. "And if he'd been more upfront with both of us, Stacey probably never would've come here. He obviously never told her about me when he broke it off with her. I mean—if it was serious enough that she planned to move here, don't you think he should've told her some *very important reasons* why those plans were no longer a good idea? I'm thinking he only told us both the bare minimum, which is kind of a cop-out."

The girls nodded and Courtney conceded. "Now I understand why you seem so upset. I mean—on top of everything else—with your job and all." She reached behind her and rubbed Gia's shoulder midstride.

The trail left the meadow and opened up to a view of the vast lake. The sky was a perfect blue to match, and they stopped to take a few group photos in front of the water. Gia brushed off the anxiety long enough to put her arms around her friends and muster a genuine smile. She was lucky to have these girls.

Kira spoke up from the back as they picked up the pace again. "So are you going to call him out on it? You guys should talk. Maybe he didn't even know she took the apartment until today?"

"Doesn't matter. He knew about the chance of it a couple of weeks ago. He could've mentioned it to me—it's a pretty big deal—if they'd made plans for her to move here.

Don't you think? And besides, if he couldn't tell me *that*—what else is he not telling me? Or what else—in the future? It makes me worry."

"Oh, yeah, I get it," Kira said. The others nodded.

"I've been burned enough times..."

"Been there, done that." Angela glanced back with a knowing look.

"I still think you should hear him out," Courtney said. "You never really know what's going on with people until you give them a chance to defend themselves. I should know."

The girls agreed, grinning. They all knew her history with Nick and how a few secrets had almost destroyed them.

Kira called out from the back. "I second the motion."

Gia was quiet for a few seconds. "I guess you guys are right. Anyway, I'd better find out if she's actually staying before I lose it, but I'm *so* dreading the answer."

"I CHANGED MY FLIGHT THIS MORNING." Stacey stared at the grass as she and Seth strolled through the orchard midday. "I fly out of Milwaukee at nine fifteen tomorrow morning. Would you mind taking me to the airport?"

He turned to gaze at her, stunned. He'd been hoping she'd do this, but he hadn't expected her to go ahead and take care of it without some persuasion on his part. "Sure. Absolutely." He nodded. It was a three-and-a-half-hour trip one way to Milwaukee and they'd have to leave long before the sun came up tomorrow, but he didn't mind. He could use the drive home to think, plus, the sooner they put this behind them, the better. "Thanks, Stace."

She looked over at him cautiously. "You think you can take me over to the apartment complex so I can pick up my suitcases today, too? I'll see if I can get out of the lease."

"Of course." Seth nodded. "Stacey, I'm sorry things are—"

"—You don't have to say anything, Seth. I know I was out of control last night. It was totally impulsive for me to jump on a plane and come here. To go ahead with plans to move here when you told me not to. I wish I had taken you at your word and listened. I'm really sorry I made such a mess of things." She hung her head.

"Thanks. Me, too." Seth cast his gaze to the ground and they continued in silence to the end of a row of cherry trees. "Listen, I owe you an apology." He took a deep breath and looked over at her. "I should've told you about Gia at some point when we talked after—well, after we broke up. You never would've thought there was any hope of us getting back together if I had, and you deserved to know. I'm sorry." He looked over at her. "And I meant it when I said I didn't cheat on you, but..." He stared back at the ground and stopped walking, so she stopped. He looked back at her. "But she and I met while you and I were still dating. We developed a friendship, and I'll be totally honest—I did start to have feelings for her before I broke it off with you. If I'd have just told you the whole truth instead of downplaying that aspect of it—"

"—You mean leaving that aspect out of it *entirely*?" Stacey started walking again and Seth followed. Her tone was dry but she seemed like she was okay with the statement.

Seth shot her an ironic smile. "Yeah, leaving it out

entirely—then you would've realized it was really over for us. I could've saved you a lot of trouble."

"—And a lot of money." Stacey snorted under her breath.

"That, too."

"And this horrible hangover."

Seth grinned. "Oh, I tried to save you from that, but you weren't havin' it."

She laughed then sighed heavily. "It's okay. You probably never thought I'd do something so impulsive."

He raised an eyebrow. "You can say that again." He stole another glance at her.

She grinned. "It's my fault, in the end. I'll take the blame."

Seth waved it off, but he appreciated the sentiment.

"And I figured you'd met someone. I knew something had changed between us a while back. I'm not blind. I was just in denial. I wish things had worked out."

Seth nodded.

"Stacey, you'll find someone. And soon, I'll bet. It just wasn't ever going to work out for us, but I know there's someone out there who's perfect for you."

"Thanks. I know. Anyway, Ronnie's been asking me out nonstop since you left." Stacey grinned.

"What? That snake." Seth was actually shocked. Ronnie was another tasting-room attendant. He'd always flirted with Stacey openly, and it always got on Seth's nerves. "Why didn't you tell me?"

Stacey laughed but didn't answer.

Seth grinned. "All right, then." Fair enough. "So have you gone out with him since we...?"

"Yeah."

Seth nodded, shocked again. "Okay..." It felt strange to

hear that, but it actually made all of this easier on both of them. He glanced back at the orchard.

"Your parents are really nice, by the way. I'm sorry I was so rude to them last night. I apologized to your mother this morning." Stacey shook her head. "I feel so awful about it all. I'm sorry I ruined the party for you."

Seth nodded. "You didn't ruin it—not the *whole* thing, anyway."

Stacey laughed again then frowned.

"Don't worry. There's no permanent damage. I talked to the guest of honor this morning. She's cool about it. She thought it was kind of funny."

Stacey turned pink. "Well, that's one way to look at it."

"Right?"

"Anyway, Seth, I'm glad I got to see you here—see this place. It's really beautiful. Even more beautiful than I imagined." She glanced around at the trees and the gleaming red barn in the distance, the blue skies overhead and the endless green in every direction, despite the ailing portion of the orchard. They stopped to listen as the cicadas hummed in the early afternoon heat.

"Thanks. I'm happy here, finally. I definitely missed my life in California for a while, but I realized I really missed *this* lifestyle. The one I grew up with. And I can make this place—and my life—whatever I want to now. It just took me a while to see that."

Stacey curved her lips. "I'm glad you're making it work. I missed you back in Sonoma. I really missed you." Her eyes grew moist and she stopped to look up at him.

Seth pulled her in for a bittersweet bear hug and held her tight as she burst into tears. "I missed you too." He had truly felt the same loss after he'd moved back—for weeks on end. He knew the pain she felt, even though those same feelings had long since dissipated for him.

"I'm glad I got to see you here too, Stace—after all those times I said I just couldn't picture you here. I was wrong about that—you look perfectly at home."

"Too late now, though," she said with an ironic smile, wiping her eyes. She started walking again.

He nodded and followed. "You'd be bored really quickly, anyway."

"I know." She stole a wry glance at him and he smiled.

They circled back to the barn and Seth gave her a tour of the wine-tasting room and the barrel room, which were open to the public for the afternoon. A few guests stood around, sipping and talking, enjoying the atmosphere.

Stacey took it all in. "It's really nice."

He was glad to see she appreciated it. "I'm going to turn it into something more. More visitors, more varieties. This is going to be an event space, too. Maybe it'll never quite reach Henderson's level, but still, it'll grow."

"I have no doubt it will." She gazed at him for a long moment. "Good luck with your farm. I'll be sure and tell everyone how great you're doing here."

"Thanks." They headed back toward the house.

"So what are you going to do? Does that mean you're going back to Henderson?"

"Yeah. The boss said I could come back if things didn't work out here. I guess he knows you better than I do."

Seth smiled. *Thank goodness for small favors.*

MONDAY MORNING ARRIVED and Gia hurried into work. She hadn't been able to find a parking spot in the lot this morning, despite the fact that she'd arrived twenty minutes earlier than usual, just for good measure, so she'd parked on a street two blocks away. With a deep breath, she inhaled the sweet and calming scent of the flowering shrubs lining the quiet sidewalk and turned up the walkway.

Her nerves were not doing her any favors this morning —that was for sure. She exhaled slowly.

Noreen would've talked to Abigail by now, most likely. Gia tossed back her hair, straightened her shoulders, and went inside.

Noreen stood in the lobby, pouring herself a cup of coffee. Gia had hoped to get here first. Too late. "Good morning, Gia."

"Good morning." Gia greeted her. "How are you today?"

"Doing fine. Yourself?" Noreen took a sip of her coffee.

Gia nodded. "I'm good."

"Why don't you get yourself situated and come into my office? We'll talk."

Gia nodded and walked to her desk. This was it. She was getting fired after all, wasn't she? No one says *we'll talk* when they have something good to say. She set her purse down and put her lunch in the community refrigerator then strode over to Noreen's office.

"Please, have a seat." Noreen gestured rigidly to the chair facing her desk, and Gia sat down.

Noreen revealed little emotion. "Abigail and I spoke yesterday afternoon." She paused for effect. "And while we weren't happy with the incident at the party, Abigail sang your praises. She said you were forced to deal with an awful personal scenario in a rather public manner, and that you handled it with grace and dignity. In fact, she said she even enjoyed the drama—the gossip kept everyone talking all night."

Gia winced but let out the breath she'd been holding, then cleared her throat. "Wow. Well, that's, uh, great to hear?" She let a smile cross her face. "Thank you?"

Noreen grinned. "Regarding the party, itself, I understand everything went extremely well. Abigail said she would be hiring us again for certain, and she would specifically request that *you* plan and run the next event. She also said they'd like to use the orchard again in the future. I told her about the winery space and she loved that idea, too. She said they'll rent out both."

Seriously? "That's wonderful."

"It really is, isn't it? So, great work, despite the tricky situation. I'm proud of you."

"Thank you, Noreen." That meant a lot.

"On that note, I have a new client whose wedding will be late next spring, and I'd like you to take the account. On your own."

"Really?" Gia's eyes lit up.

"Really. I'll let you get started with your day now, and we'll meet about it later this afternoon so I can go over the details with you. She's coming in this week to meet with us."

Gia stood up to leave. "That sounds great! Oh, thank you so much, Noreen. I really appreciate it." It was finally happening! That carrot was hers.

"You've earned it, Gia. But one more thing—I understand you're dating Seth Pederson now, and I don't have a problem with that, but don't let your personal life get in the way of your work again. You might not get so lucky next time." She shot her a wry look.

Gia nodded and shut Noreen's door behind her.

Whew.

TWENTY-ONE

Late Monday afternoon, Seth rolled back into town. It had been a long trip to Milwaukee and back. He and Stacey had chatted and laughed on the way to the airport, reminiscing about old times. They'd talked some more about how things had changed between them, and she said she finally understood why her plan to move there never would've worked in the long run. She'd even told Seth to tell Gia she was sorry for the way she'd behaved at the party. Seth thanked her and promised her he would.

He glanced at the lake as he drove down Main Street in Heritage Bay. The good news was, he'd learned his lesson—that he needed to take the initiative in his relationships, not rely on the wait-and-see approach. He also needed to trust his gut even when the outcome of the situation would make him uncomfortable. Gia had asked him to be more transparent with her in the future, and he promised himself he'd do that, too.

The bad news was, he'd made a huge mess of things by trying to dodge the details with both women. He only hoped he hadn't lost Gia in the process.

She still hadn't returned his calls. She had, at least, texted him back yesterday, telling him she wasn't ready to discuss anything while Stacey was still here. He told her he understood. He just wished she'd talk to him.

She had every right to be upset. Stacey had been extremely rude to her and he'd put Gia in a very difficult position, as much as he'd tried to avoid it all evening.

But she was right. He needed to close out the Stacey part of his life entirely before he could give Gia everything that he wanted to. She deserved that from him, at the very least.

He cursed himself as he turned off the main road onto a side street, wondering how he was going to make it right with her. First things first, though—isn't that what people always said?

The sprawling apartment complex where Stacey had rented the unit appeared on his right, and he steered into the lot. He parked outside the rental office, which had been closed yesterday when he and Stacey came by. He'd held onto Stacey's key, promising he'd return it for her today.

He hopped out of the truck, went inside, and approached the receptionist behind the counter. "Hi. Is there a manager around that I can talk to about terminating a lease early?"

"Sure. I'll get someone out here for you, if you'll just have a seat." She gestured politely to the chairs by the window.

"Thanks." Seth sat down.

A couple of minutes later, Tom came into the lobby and held out a hand to shake. "Hey, Seth." He smiled.

Seth stood up and frowned. "Tom." He hadn't necessarily expected to see Tom. Sure, there was a chance of it, but he was hoping he'd get someone who didn't already have a bone to pick with him. "Good to see you again," he lied.

"Come on." Tom gestured with a nod and Seth followed him to his office. Tom closed the door behind them. "Have a seat."

Tom didn't seem angry and his voice wasn't particularly threatening, as it had been the night of the bonfire, but Seth could only imagine what Tom must think of him now. Gia had probably talked to him since Saturday night and told him what had happened. Seth sat back, rested one foot on a knee, and painted the most reasonable expression he could manage across his face.

"So what can I do for you?"

Seth cleared his throat and tapped his fingers on the chair. "As you probably know, my, uh, ex-girlfriend rented a place here the other day. She signed the papers on Saturday." He set the key on the desk in front of Tom. "She left this morning for California. She's hoping to terminate her lease immediately without a penalty, if there's any way you'd consider it. She's on a plane right now so I promised her I'd stop by and see what your office had to say. We tried yesterday but you were, obviously, closed."

Tom's brow shot up and he sat back in his high-backed leather chair, nodding. "Hmm." He scrubbed a hand over the stubble on his chin then sat up. "Yeah, that's not a problem. I'll return her security deposit and the full month's rent, in full."

Seth sat forward. "You will?" He'd figured Tom would've given him a hard time. What was going on here?

"Sure." He nodded agreeably.

"Thanks. I really appreciate that," Seth said cautiously then gazed at him for a long second. "Are we cool, man? I know things were a bit off between us last time I saw you."

"We're cool, yeah." Tom sat forward. "So Stacey's gone, huh? Just like that?" He snapped his fingers.

"Yeah. It's over between us. Has been for a long time. She never should've rented the place. I'm really sorry we wasted your time."

Tom waved it off. "No worries, man." He stared at the desk for a second. "But you and Gia—and I apologize for getting personal here, but she's a good friend of mine. She told me about Saturday night."

Seth nodded. "Yeah, I made a huge mess of things. There are a lot of things I should've done differently. I was so stupid..." He ran a hand across his forehead and rubbed it over his eyes.

Tom brushed it off. "We've all been there, dude, but I have to ask you—are you going to make things right with her?"

Seth opened his eyes wider and stared back at Tom for a second. "I'm going to try my best, but I don't even know if she'll give me another chance. She hasn't returned my calls." He cast his gaze to the floor. "I care about her. I can't lose her."

Tom gazed at him. "You know, I thought you were bad news for her, but I think maybe I was wrong."

Seth gazed at him, surprised. "Thanks."

"Don't screw this up, dude. She's one in a million."

Seth stared at him then stood up. "Yes, she is."

Tom stood and held out a hand, and Seth shook.

Seth met his gaze. "Thanks a lot, dude. I really appreciate your help with the apartment—and with everything else."

"No worries," Tom said lightly. "I'll see you around."

LATER THAT AFTERNOON, Gia walked into her apartment after work, and her phone rang from inside her purse. She'd been planning to call her mother back tonight. They'd talked about the party yesterday after the hike, and her mother said she'd check on her today. It was probably her.

She took the phone out and saw Tom's name on the screen, instead. "Hey, Tom." She set her keys on the counter and a stack of mail next to them.

"Hey, Gia. How's it going? You doin' any better?"

"Yeah, thanks. Much better than the other night." She told him about the new account at work and how the client had praised the way she'd handled the fiasco on Saturday. She also told him how Abigail had enjoyed the gossip they'd created and Tom laughed.

She leafed through the junk mail and bills as he talked. "I'm so glad, and congratulations on the account," Tom said. "Hey, so I had a visit from someone you know today."

"Oh, yeah? Who?" Gia's brow furrowed.

"You know who."

Gia hesitated. "Seth?" She set the envelopes back down on the counter.

"Uh-huh."

"Really?" This was certainly a surprise. "What about?"

"The Wicked Witch of the West took to her broom and flew home today. We let her out of the lease without a fee and gave her back the rest of her money."

Gia laughed. "Oh, wow. That was nice of you." She walked over to the kitchen table and took a dirty plate to the sink. "So she's really gone? Just like that?"

"Just like that. Seth stopped in to drop off the key." Tom stopped talking for a second or two. "He's a good dude, Gia. He did the right thing here. I know you're upset with him, but he has your best interest at heart. I can see it now."

"What makes you say that? I thought you couldn't stand him?"

"Nothing really, except that we talked—just enough that I could see it in him, plain as day. When I sat down and thought about it later, I realized he didn't do anything worse than I did. He left out some very important information to try to simplify things—he thought it was no big deal, and it backfired on him, just like it backfired on me when I didn't tell you what I knew about the apartment. And you gave *me* another chance."

Gia thought about that. Tom had a point.

"He seems really sorry to me, and I'm not the one dating him."

Gia chuckled.

"You should give him a chance. As much as it pains me to say this, I think you guys are perfect for each other."

Gia's jaw dropped. A couple of seconds passed. This was pretty huge.

"You still there?"

"Yeah, I'm here. Just a little shocked you'd say that."

"Right? Last week I wanted to strangle him. This week I'm playing Cupid for the guy."

Gia laughed. "What's gotten into you, Garcia?"

"Well, you know I wouldn't be saying it if I didn't mean it. You should call him. Both of you deserve to be happy."

Gia nodded even though Tom couldn't see her. Tears moistened her eyes. "Wow. Thanks, Tom. Hugs."

Tom paused for a second. "Back at ya, kid."

SETH SAT ALONE behind the barn on Tuesday evening in the same chair he'd sat in after the festival a few weeks ago. He stared into the distance at the orchard, remembering how beautiful Gia looked sitting next to him by candlelight, how caught up he'd been in talking with her. How perfect a night that had been, even though it had been perfectly platonic.

Would he ever get to sit here with her again? Or had the other night taken away the magic between them? Had Gia decided she just wasn't interested anymore? A guy with too much baggage and a lousy track record for handling his personal life. What a mess the other night had been. He shook his head. For a night that had started out so perfectly, it sure had ended in chaos.

He'd left her another message this afternoon, but she still hadn't answered. How ironic would it be if things were over between them now? He'd finally made things right with his ex and both of them could move on properly, but he may have lost the woman he was falling in love with.

He stared at the hazy yellow sky and propped his feet up on a chair. Probably about half an hour until sunset. He leaned back, shaking his head. He glanced over at the seat Gia had occupied and wondered what it would take to win her back. Would she be willing to listen if he asked her to? He *had* to explain.

He picked his phone up from the table and dialed her number. There was no way he was going to let her go over this. She picked up on the first ring.

"Hey," he said, surprised she'd taken his call at last.

"Hey, yourself," she said sweetly.

"What are you up to?" he asked. She didn't sound upset.

"Not much. You?"

"I'm just sitting out back behind the winery, thinking about you."

Her voice went up a few scales. "Really? That's funny because I was just thinking about *you*." Her voice over the phone sounded like maybe she was out walking.

"Really?" He crossed one foot over the other and sat back.

"So what were you thinking—about me?" Gia asked.

"Well, for starters, I was hoping you'd give me a chance to tell you how much I miss you."

"Oh yeah, how much do you miss me?" She sounded almost playful.

"More than you know." His heart began to beat faster and then he turned, confused. Suddenly her voice was coming from not just the phone, but...

He glanced around. There she was, on the other side of the patio. She must've just come around the corner of the barn. He hung up the phone and wasted no time reaching her. "You're here," he said quietly, eyes wide.

"I am." She ended the call and smiled up at him tenderly. "I miss you, too. A lot."

This was actually happening? He could hardly believe it. He smiled and picked her up and spun her around, and she laughed. He set her down in front of him, but she kept her arms around his neck. He leaned down and kissed her softly on the lips and she kissed him back eagerly.

"What made you come here?" he asked.

Gia looked into his eyes. "Someone I trust convinced me I ought to give you another shot."

Tom. He'd intervened again, huh? He really was a good friend to her. To both of them. "I think I know who you mean," he said.

She nodded. "He told me about the apartment—how he knew about it weeks ago. And then about the job, the other day."

Seth cast his gaze to the ground. "I should've told you about it—right after we started dating. You asked me to be up front with you—to be more honest, and I wasn't. I'm so sorry, Gia."

She raised his chin and looked into his eyes then kissed him again. "That's exactly what I needed to hear you say. I mean—I wouldn't have been quite so caught off guard when she showed up if I'd have known about that."

He nodded. "I know. I screwed up all around—I should've been more honest with her, too. She never would've come here if I'd have told her about you in the first place. I mean—she can come *unglued* sometimes over little things, but she wouldn't have been out for blood. This whole thing could've been prevented. I really handled it badly."

Gia took each of his hands in hers and he squeezed them. She smelled so amazing. He'd missed her so badly, it hurt.

"I'm so sorry about your job, too. So what happened at work today?" He shot her a look of concern.

Gia smiled, her eyes wide. "Guess what? Noreen gave me a wedding. I get to plan and run it from start to finish. Noreen said if this had been a test, then I passed with flying colors. I'll be getting more accounts of my own now!"

"Really? That's so great!" So Abigail had come through for him. *Whew.* He gave her another hug.

Gia squeezed him tightly. "She also said that Abigail wants to use your winery space here too, sometime."

He pulled back for a better look at her. Gia was so beautiful—it made his heart ache. "Really? That's fantastic!" Seth wrapped his arms around her again and spoke softly. "Gia, I'm so sorry about everything. I want to fix things with you. I want to prove I can give you what you need. I want to pick up where we left off before Stacey showed up. Whatever it takes, I just... I just want *you*."

Gia pulled back to gaze into his eyes then wrapped her arms around his neck and kissed him passionately. After the kiss, she spoke softly into his ear. "That's why I'm here," she said. "I want that, too."

Seth relaxed.

She pulled back again. "But listen, I have to take some of the blame. I knew what was going on with Stacey the other night, and I should've stayed out of the way. If I hadn't been acting so needy, Ryan Trewet never would've seen that kiss between us and nothing would've happened. Stacey never would've been the wiser. Everything would've been fine."

Seth shook his head. "You weren't acting needy." He ran a hand gently through her hair.

"Well, I felt like I was. When I saw you dancing with her—I just... I couldn't get past it, and I needed reassurance."

So that was it. He hadn't realized it had bothered her so much. Of course it did, though—duh. Why hadn't that occurred to him? It would've bothered him if the situation had been reversed. "No, you definitely weren't acting needy, but whatever was going on, I'm glad it happened."

GIA GAZED AT HIM. "What do you mean—you're glad?" It worked out in the end, but she'd have been perfectly happy if the whole debacle had never happened.

"I'm sure that the whole thing was really difficult on you, and you barely knew what was going on—that it was all just an act for me, with her, all night. I felt awful, putting you through that. I was trying to keep her from ruining your big night, though. Mine, too."

Gia cast her gaze to the ground. "I know. That's why I feel bad. You were just doing what you had to do."

"But it made me face what I needed to do, which was work things out with Stacey, give her some closure, and move past that relationship and the mistakes I made. I'm actually glad that Stacey knows about us now. It felt so much better to be honest with her. She left here on a good note. She won't be hounding me anymore because she knows it wouldn't have worked out for us now. As painful as it is sometimes, you're right—honesty *is* best."

Gia's mouth turned up on one side and she looked back up at him. *He gets it now. He really gets it.* She nodded and kissed him again.

Seth stepped back and held out his hand. "Hey, come over here," he said sweetly. "We have some unfinished business to take care of."

"We do? What unfinished business?" Gia followed him across the winery's patio.

They reached the table where Seth's phone sat and he dropped her hand gently. He picked up the phone and tapped at it for a few seconds before a popular love song began to play from it. Then he set the phone back down on the table and lit the citronella candle that he'd brought out earlier. He held out his hand again. "Will you dance with me?"

Gia's face broke into a big smile. "I'd love to." She took his hand.

He pulled her in close, and she wrapped her arms around his neck. He locked his hands behind her waist, and they swayed to the music.

Could any man be more perfect than Seth was? She doubted it.

The sun dropped behind the trees as Gia rested her head on his chest. She closed her eyes and felt the stillness all around them. Strength, compassion, the ability to admit and atone for his mistakes—Seth was truly everything she ever wanted in a man, and more.

She breathed him in and squeezed her arms tightly around him. He understood her, and she was beginning to understand him. She'd never get enough of him.

When the song ended, she pulled back and looked him in the eyes. "Seth, I want you, too. I want *this*. I want to pick up right where we left off, just like you said."

Seth pulled her close again and she felt the intensity of whatever he was about to say. He looked into her eyes. "I'm going to do better this time. I'm going to try *everyday* to make you as happy as you've made me. I'm falling in love with you, Gia. I'm falling hard."

She caught her breath and gazed at him. She felt the same way. Her heart was bursting. This was real and she wanted to give him everything. She placed her hand softly on his cheek. "I'm in love with you, too, Seth. Completely in love with you."

THE END

ACKNOWLEDGMENTS

I would like to thank my family for their constant love and undying support.

I would like to thank my editor and all of my critique partners and beta readers who so generously took the time and patience to read my manuscript and share their honest opinions with me.

And I'd like to thank you, readers, for taking the time to read my book! I hope you enjoyed reading it as much as I enjoyed writing it! Please consider leaving me a review. I would love to hear from you!

Don't miss out on any **One Sweet Day** news and releases! Stop on by and join my email list at JillianWalshRomance.com

ABOUT THE AUTHOR

Jillian Walsh writes clean, feel-good, sweet romance with heart. She's been weaving stories inside her head for decades. Fortunately, nowadays, she writes them down. Fall in love with her heartfelt characters, soak up her dreamy, vacation-like settings, and get caught up in her escapist PG reads. JillianWalshRomance.com

Follow Jillian Walsh on social media:

Made in the USA
Monee, IL
27 January 2023